*The Heavens Opened* is an amazing and beautiful revelation of the place that He has gone to prepare for us and where we will spend eternity. Of the many recent books written about our future home, none reveal so clearly the glory of God that awaits us if we are faithful to Him during the days of testing that many have already begun to experience. You will read it more than once, and you will want to share it with all your friends. You will not be able to put it down!

*—Gwen Shaw*
*End-Time Handmaidens*

In this exciting book, Anna Rountree will help to take you beyond the veil into a realm where holiness, obedience, and unconditional surrender are the qualifications that will take you into the very presence of the Lord. She shares the importance of living a life of worship that has caused the heavens to be opened in her own personal life, bringing fresh understanding of the angelic realm that has also taken her into the very throne room of God.

*—Suzanne Hinn*

# The Heavens Opened

## Anna Rountree

**Charisma**
**HOUSE**
A STRANG COMPANY

THE HEAVENS OPENED by Anna Rountree
Published by Charisma House
A Strang Company
600 Rinehart Road
Lake Mary, Florida 32746
www.charismahouse.com

Unless otherwise noted, all Scripture quotations are from the New American Standard Bible. Copyright © 1960, 1962, 1963, 1968, 1971, 1972, 1973, 1975, 1977 by the Lockman Foundation. Used by permission.

Scripture quotations marked KJV are from the King James Version of the Bible.

Scripture quotations marked AMP are from the Amplified Bible. Old Testament copyright © 1965, 1987 by the Zondervan Corporation. The Amplified New Testament copyright © 1954, 1958, 1987 by the Lockman Foundation. Used by permission.

Scripture quotations marked JB are from the Jerusalem Bible. Copyright © 1966 by Darton, Longman, and Todd, Ltd. and Doubleday, a division of Random House, Inc. Used by permission.

**Library of Congress Cataloging-in-Publication Data**
Rountree, Anna.
  The heavens opened / by Anna Rountree.
    p. cm.
  ISBN: 0-88419-598-8
  I. Title.
PS3568.08875H43  1999
813'.54—dc21                                                    98-40738
                                                                      CIP

06 07 08 09 — 11 10 9 8
*Printed in the United States of America*

*To God the Father,*
*God the Son, and God the Holy Spirit,*
*who gave the revelation, commissioned the book,*
*and to whom we offer it in love,*
*praise, and thanksgiving.*

*Truly, truly I say to you,*
*you shall see the heavens opened…*

—John 1:51

# Contents

～✸～

*The revelations are best experienced
by reading the narrative straight through to the
end and then studying the Notes.*

# 1

# The Attack

THE SOUND WAS ancient and terrifying.

Startled, I spun around to see a colossal battering ram relentlessly moving under its own power across a desert basin.[1] Its wooden wheels were at least sixty stories high, and they groaned and yawned under the extreme weight they bore. Blasphemies were carved into its black battering arm, the end of which was the iron head of a goat.[2]

Although it moved slowly, people on the desert floor seemed helpless to avoid its path; they were crushed as it rolled over them.[3] Screams filled the desert valley and ricocheted off distant rock formations, filling the desert basin with terror.

Slowly the battering ram topped a sandy hill and began to pick up speed going down the other side. Breathless from shock, I clawed with my hands and dug with my feet into the deep sand of the hill in order to reach the top and watch its path.

It picked up tremendous speed as it plunged down the other side of the hill into a deep valley. In its path at the bottom of the hill was a walled city. Both city and wall were the color of the sand and seemed to be half sunk into it, almost reclaimed by the sand from which they had come. In faded lettering on the side of the wall, I could read: THE CHURCH.[4]

The battering ram was massive, and the adobe wall of the city did not look strong. With brutal impact, the goat's head smashed into the wall and continued through it. It plowed through houses and buildings, losing little of its speed. When it broke through the wall on the opposite side of the city, it slowed to a stop, settling into the sand.

A strange silence fell.

Occasional screams broke this silence. They came from those who had been mutilated or from those who recognized that a loved one had been killed. But stranger than the silence was the fact that few sought to escape across the rubble of the wall—few.

Then slowly, all by itself, the battering ram turned and began to start up the hill again, moving in my direction. The goat's head on the end of the ram was laughing, exhilarated, as if drunk with blood.

I thought it might see me, so I left the top of the hill and began to run in the opposite direction. As I ran, I frantically scanned the desert basin for a hiding place. I could hear the huge wheels laboring as they carried the battering ram toward the top of the hill again.

Suddenly an angel began to fly beside me.

"Where can I hide from the battering ram?" I shouted as I ran.

"The battering ram rolls relentlessly over all the earth now. Up high," the angel said, "up higher than it can see is the only safe place. Let me show you."

# The Attack

## The Escape

WITH A WAVE of the angel's hand, a stairway appeared, touching the earth and reaching beyond my view into heaven.[5] I moved to the base of the stairs and looked up. I was still heaving from running.

The angel flew beside the stairs, higher than its base on earth, and waved me upward: "Come on!" the angel shouted. "The ram is coming, and we don't want him to see this stairway. Come on!"

There were no hand rails on the narrow stairs. The stairs were clear like glass, which can be slippery. I could hear the battering ram rolling; although I was still panting, I began to run up the stairs.

"Faster!" the angel called.

I kept my eyes on the stairs. In his hands the angel had a scarlet cord fastened to the stairs at the bottom.[6] I could hear the battering ram getting closer, but the angel pulled the cord and brought up the first section of the stairway, like attic stairs that can be lowered and raised.

"Hurry!" the angel urged.

I continued to run up the steps, breathless. The angel pulled the thin rope, and another section of the stairs rose.

"Keep climbing," the angel said, although now his tone of voice was less urgent.

With a mighty effort, I completed the stairs and turned to make sure I had indeed escaped. The battering ram was directly below, rolling beneath us as the third section of the stairs was pulled up.

"You were safe after climbing the second set of stairs; but to be *really* safe, you needed to pass the third,"[7–8] he said.

As the battering ram rolled past, I tried to catch my breath and settle myself. Only then did I look around.

"Where am I?" I asked.

## Paradise

"PARADISE," THE ANGEL smiled, as he tied the cord holding the stairs to a docking post.[9] A sign above the post read STAIRPORT.

I looked out over the most beautiful park I had ever seen. There were gentle rolling hills, beds of subtly colored flowers, and grass as uniform and green as the rolled lawns of English manor houses. A walking path crossed this part of the park. There were also quiet pools, a stream, and luxuriant trees that on earth would have provided shade, but there was no shade or any shadows here. A soft light emanated from everything growing.

*Beautiful,* I thought.

"Yes, isn't it," the angel answered.

I did not seem surprised that he read my thoughts. I turned to look at him; only then did his appearance register with me. He looked to be six feet two or six feet three inches in height and in his mid-thirties, if I were gauging by human years. He had brown curly hair and wore a brown, transparent, full-length robe. Underneath the thin brown robe, I could see that he had on blue-and-white-striped work overalls, the sort one might obtain in the store of a farming community. The thought struck me that the brown over-robe was so thin that it was probably cool to wear when working.

A coil of rope crossed his shoulder and chest, circled in a wide loop near his waist, and returned across his back to the shoulder again. He wore a white belt, from which hung a white tool pouch. This pouch looked a little like the handtool belt worn by telephone repairers. He was unlacing a pair of silver-tipped, brown, hightopped work boots as he spoke to me.

"No shoes up here," he smiled. "This is holy ground."[10] I looked down at my own feet and saw that they, too, were bare.

He stood up, putting the boots under his arm. "You're safe here," the angel continued, "All of that is down below."

"What was that?" I asked.

"The great enemy of our Lord and of His church."

"But it was *destroying* the church," I exclaimed.

## The Two Churches

"SOME OF IT may be destroyed—that which *calls* itself the

church," he continued. "It has a sign saying it is the church, and many live behind that sign. But the church—*the real church*—escaped; the real church is alive and can run faster than any battering ram can roll. It's clumsy, really; but if you are dead stones, if you are not alive, then of course it is more than any man-made structure can resist. However, the real, living church of Jesus Christ can hide in caves, float on the water, or climb into Paradise.[11] A member of the real church will know where the hidden stairs are located. That person can call for help, and we will let down the stairs so that he can escape. The real church is more agile than the battering ram. Living stones have feet."

Then, like someone who had just remembered his manners, he said, "Would you like some refreshments? It would help you."

"All right," I said, trying to get my bearings.

A tray of fruit floated to us.[12] "Here you are," the angel said, gesturing toward the tray, "a choice."

I reached to make a selection of fruit. Some varieties I had seen on earth, and some I had not. All were without blemish. We both made selections and began to eat.[13]

"You need to get acquainted with the locations of the hidden stairs," he continued.

"Is there a map?" I asked.

"No," the angel laughed. "The map is in the Spirit. By following His leading, He directs you to the hidden stairs."

I glanced toward the stairport. "These stairs look like glass," I said.

"Light," the angel replied.[14] "Nice, aren't they?"

"Do people ever fall off these stairs?"

"Not if they keep their eyes on Jesus," he chuckled, "but I wouldn't advise looking over the side. You might get wobbly doing that."

"This is good fruit," I exclaimed.

"Yup, everything's good up here," the angel said, mimicking a cowhand.

I laughed, bemused. He was not anything like my idea of an angel. "What is your name?" I asked him.

## The Angel Azar

"AZAR," THE ANGEL said, "I'm the one who answers when you call for help."[15]

"Is there only one of you?" I asked.

"You mean for the whole earth? Oh no, I couldn't take care of the whole earth. We're assigned to a small number to whose call we will respond, more or less according to lifestyle. Sometimes a stunt person will need one of us all by him or herself, but usually we can handle five. The boss chooses who they will be."

"The boss?" I said.

"Well, our immediate boss, not the Lord; no, I mean the angel in charge of helps. While you are living on earth, I'm the one who will answer your call for help. So don't take up mountain climbing," he laughed.

He amazed me.

"Had enough fruit?" he asked.

"Yes, thank you," I said. The tray of fruit disappeared.

## The Suggestion

"NOW," THE ANGEL continued, "you can return the way you came. The present danger is past, but I would suggest that you take the path to the throne room. You must be here for a reason, but that knowledge has not been given to me.[16] Your Father can tell you why you have come."

"My Father?" I said, glancing out into the park, lost in reflection. It seemed inconceivable, not only that I was in Paradise, but also that I could go to see my heavenly Father as a child might go to see an earthly one.

"Certainly," he said, reading my thoughts. "Just take the path."

"Does this path lead to the throne room?"

"All paths here lead to God. They are not like the paths on earth."

I looked toward the path as if it were a distant horizon too far away to reach.

"Go on," he laughed. "Go see your Daddy. I'll be here when it's time for you to return."

I turned to search his face.

"Don't you want to know why you're here?" he asked.

"Yes," I laughingly exclaimed.

He threw up his hands and shrugged, as if to say, "Well?"

"Thank you," I said earnestly.

He smiled at me and spoke quietly, "The Creator of the universe desires your company. Don't keep Him waiting."

I smiled and showed him that I was stepping onto the path.

He called after me, "I'll be here when it's time to return."

I waved to him, acknowledging that I had heard. Then, somewhat breathlessly, I set my face toward the throne room.

2

# Sandcastles

**M**UCH TO MY amazement, the path on which I had begun to walk seemed to be in motion, like a conveyor belt or a moving sidewalk. I looked down at my bare feet standing on its smooth, advancing surface.[1]

It was then that I noticed another pair of feet beside mine. I was not traveling alone. I looked up into the face of a large angel.

"Hello," he said formally.

"Hello," I answered. He was about seven feet tall, with blonde hair that seemed to have lights in it. Perhaps the light was within him and shone out through his head and then his hair. I could not tell. His face was grave with the demeanor of authority.

He wore a long white robe and had large, strong, white wings.
"Who are you?" I continued.

## Angel of Promises

"I AM A messenger," the angel replied.[2]

I could feel power emanating from him. "What kind of messages do you deliver?" I asked.

"Promises," he said. "I help to bring God's faithful promises to mankind."[3]

"That's a big job," I quipped. (I was hoping he'd become less formal.)

"Very," he nodded stiffly.

He didn't. *So,* I thought, *perhaps all angels are not alike. This spirit is very serious, like an ambassador.* Suddenly I remembered that he knew what I was thinking.[4] "Have you been delivering promises on earth?" I asked aloud.

"Yes," he said, pausing to weigh his words, "yours."

"Mine!" I exclaimed.

"Yours," he reiterated. "When you came into the kingdom, the Lord told you that you would see into heaven, did He not?"

"Yes," I answered vaguely, looking out over the passing landscape. I was searching my memory. "That was years ago."

## The Promise

WHEN I CAME to the Lord twenty years before, it was a time of miracles. At that time He spoke to me several promises that related to my life on earth. Although I did not keep these pledges in the forefront of my thoughts, I realized that He was fulfilling most of them daily. But this one promise, this amazing promise, had not been fulfilled. At first I looked and longed for its fulfillment; after a time, however, immediate demands crowded out anticipation until truly I had forgotten. "Nothing happened," I continued, "and..." My voice trailed off. I started to say that I had forgotten.

"However, God has not forgotten," he said, "and the fullness of time has come."

I hardly heard him for I was trying to piece together the past with this present.

"Being ignorant of God's ways does not negate their functioning," he said. "Of course, great unbelief does hinder."[5]

"But what does it mean?" I asked, searching his face.

"I do not have the authority to tell you. Ask your Father. The Revealer of Mysteries will reveal this mystery to you."[6]

I was lost in the wonder of it, so he continued, "Our God is faithful and true, and He loves you."

It seems that at times of great impact or distress, one can think of the most unusual things. Suddenly I wanted to know his name. "What is your name?" I asked.

"Seek for me in Scripture. Your Father wishes you to grow in confirmation from the written Word of all that you see and hear.[7] Seek for my name," he said, and then he was gone.

## The Tour

BEFORE I COULD adjust to his sudden disappearance, I heard the distinct sound of a voice projected through a megaphone, as on a bus tour: "Pleasant hills, soft turf, cool streams..."

I turned to see a winged angel deftly weaving in and out of people farther ahead of me on the moving path, sort of like a ticket collector on a merry-go-round. He too had on a white robe, but on his head was a blue hat on which was embroidered TOUR GUIDE. Around his waist was a silver belt from which hung a silver coin exchanger. However, I never saw him ask anyone for the price of the tour.[8] His voice was high and as loud as a barker at a fair; he was pointing out areas of interest in Paradise. "All streams flow from beneath the throne.[9] All proceed from the same source," he said, weaving through a group of people. "We'll stop here so that you can enjoy this site."

The moving path stopped, and people farther up the line got off to look at the view. The tour guide turned to answer someone's question, so I too got off, walked over to a stream, and sat beside it. It was the first time I had been able to look more closely at the flora of Paradise.

The grass looked like grass, but its properties were undeniably different. You could walk on it, and it would return to its former position once the pressure had been removed from it.[10] There were several, formal plantings of flower beds near the stream, but again, these were not flowers as we know them on earth. They were perfect.

I stretched out my whole body at the water's edge and put my hand into the stream. Cool. *But, is it water?* I asked myself. *No,* I thought, *I believe it's light.* A group of angels passed overhead. They were flying in a wedge formation like a flock of geese. When I returned to look at the water, another face was looking into the stream with me.

## The Sand Pile

"HELLO," A CHILD'S voice said.

I turned and sat up to face her.

"Are you on tour?" she asked.

"Yes," I answered, staring at her. She appeared to be a child of about five or six years old, but she was shining. She had no wings, and her eyes looked old beyond the years displayed in her small stature. She wore a pale calico pinafore over a faintly colored, short shift. Her hair was curly and tousled as if from play. She looked like a little girl, but every so often I could see through her arm or leg and knew her to be a spirit. She was intriguing.

"Have you just begun the tour?" she questioned.

"Yes, I think so. Why?" I asked.

"I wanted you to come play with me," she said.

"Play with you?" I said incredulously.

"In my sand pile," she said. "Can you come?"

Just then the tour guide walked over to us, and I stood. I was torn between getting to know this small spirit and continuing my tour.

"May I go with...what is your name?" I asked her, bending

over to question her as one might question a child.

"Crystal Clear."[11]

"May I go with Crystal Clear for a few minutes?" I asked the tour guide.

"Oh, all right," he said. "Meet us at the almond grove when you finish."

"How will I find it?" I asked.

"Crystal Clear will show you the way."

"Yes, I will," she said excitedly. "Come along with me."

## The Lesson

SUDDENLY WE WERE on a vast shore line, but there was no sea.[12] It looked as though the beach was still there, but no ocean. In the sand were all manner of red and blue children's buckets and shovels.

"Haven't you always wanted to build a sand castle?" she asked.[13]

I chuckled, "Well, not really, Crystal Clear."

"Yes, you have," she continued. "Think about it. You've wanted to build on earth, and all of that is sand.[14] When the tide comes in, it goes away. Even the tools for building remain longer than a sandcastle, for the tools are from God. But if you use them to build on sand instead of in eternity, what do you have? A waste of time," she shrugged. "You have wanted a sandcastle. It's silly really, isn't it?"

"I suppose so," I said quietly. I did not want to admit it, but she was right. I had wanted a home and financial security and to accomplish something—for God, of course—but I had tunnel vision for the life on earth. I had Christianized the gospel of the world and bought into my own packaging. It was a bitter thing to hear that the focus of my life had been fleshly and worthless to God, and that I had not gotten away with it.[15]

"Do you want to play?" she continued cheerily.

I felt a little sick. I thought I would change the subject. "Why such a large sand area?" I asked.

"Many want to build on sand, so we let them. It gets it out

of their systems, you know. Maybe if you build on the sand right now, you would feel, 'I've done that.'"

"It seems a silly thing to do," I said stonily.

"Well, yes, it does. However, building on the earth is really the same: silly toys that are long forgotten here, toys that do not even gather dust in the attic but disintegrate and are totally forgotten here—a waste of God's precious time," she said much too breezily.

I had the taste of a copper penny in my mouth.[16] "Is it all right if we do not play today?" I asked.

"Oh, all right," she said. "Do you want to join the tour?"

"I don't know," I said dazed. I felt as though I had been hit by a truck. "I like your name, Crystal Clear," I said acidly. "It's apt."

"Maybe a little rest," she said, as if she had not heard my remark. "Now, remember to come back to see us. We love you here; do keep in touch." She held up her tiny hands, and I held up mine to reciprocate. Light came from hers into mine and knocked me softly backwards.[17]

I lay on the air, as someone might lie on a gurney while being wheeled through hospital halls. My arms were across my chest, and I floated down the path like a patient returning from surgery.

3

~×~

# Angels in Training

A N ANGEL BEGAN walking beside me as I floated down the path.

"Whom do you seek?" the angel asked.

"I thought I was going to see my Father in the throne room," I answered.

"He is everywhere, but this is not the throne room."

### The Terraced Waterfall

I HAD FLOATED to the edge of a pool; I began descending to rest on the grass. The pool was at the base of a high, terraced waterfall. Lavender flowers and hanging greenery grew on the ledges of the fall. A fine mist hung over the pool, caused by the impact of the falling water.

"What is this place?" I asked.

"One of the gardens," the angel said. "It's peaceful here. Why don't you rest," he suggested, and then he was gone.

There was something soothing in the sound of the waterfall, something restful, but there was also someone humming a lovely melody. The sound vibrated through me, touching every part of my body. Then a high voice began to sing:

> There is a place where travelers rest,
> And lay their heads in peace.
> Returning to the Eagle's nest,
> All war within will cease.
> O Lamb of God,
> Our heart's desire,
> O Truth in Word,
> Eternal Fire,
> O Lamb of God,
> God's chosen Son,
> Receive them when
> Their race is run.

At the song's end, slowly a figure formed from the mist of the waterfall. I sat up to watch this unusual sight.

## Heather of the Mist

"WHO ARE YOU?" I asked.

"I am Heather," the figure said. "I tend this part of the garden. Sometimes the path leads beside still waters or into perfumed gardens," she smiled.

I lay back on the grass, for I was weary and still recovering from my experience at the sand pile.

She continued after a pause, "Do you wish to grow in spirit or in the natural?"

"In spirit, most of all," I said.

"Then cultivate obedience," she said.[1] "Your Father loves you. I know that, or you would not be here. You would not have access to Him nor be able to enter these perfumed gardens."

"Tell me of these gardens," I said.

"There are many, each filled with untold delights. I suppose, being on the path, you always expect to arrive in the throne room?" she asked.

"Yes, I do."

"But your Father wants you to see more of His beautiful land."

## The Question

SUDDENLY I SAT up, looking at her intently. "Heather, what do you do here?"

"We grow in God.[2] Also, I tend this small part of the garden. But we do not toil here.[3] We live for what you would call spiritual growth." Then returning to the subject she was addressing before my question, she swept her hand in a wide semicircle. "The areas to visit are without end and beyond compare."

"I seem to be alone here," I said, "but I know there are others."[4]

"Yes, but your Father is answering your prayers to grow and learn. He decides how each child should be taught," she smiled. "For you there is private tutoring here.[5] One on one. Ask what you will."

"I'm so at peace in this place," I shrugged. "I find it difficult to think of things to ask."[6]

"I've heard that," she mused.

I could think of one question only, for which I felt I already knew the answer, but I asked: "Do you have fellowship here?"

"Yes, we are happy. Actually, there are many of us around, but I alone am sent to you, so you see only me."

"Why are you called Heather?" I asked.

"For the flowers that grow in the midst of the falls," she smiled, looking up at the high, terraced garden.

# Angels in Training

## The Angel Clara

"HELLO, ANN," A woman's voice spoke from behind us. "Heather," the voice continued, as we turned our faces toward her.

"Clara," Heather responded; she quickly rose to face her. Heather turned to me. "This is Clara, who is very beloved of us here."

I rose to my feet also. "Hello, Clara," I said. She was absolutely the most beautiful creature I had ever seen. This angel looked very womanly and had a soft light coming from her head area. The light seemed to gather into streaks of light as it radiated outward from that glow. She parted her botticellian, golden-red hair in the center and caught it in a multiple bun arrangement at the nape of her neck. She wore a white, draped garment similar to the designs adopted by Roman women before the time of Christ. The garment was gathered and belted beneath what would be the bust area in a human. Her eyes were an intense blue.

## Clara's Invitation

"I'VE COME TO take Ann to a training session," Clara continued.

"What kind of training?" I asked.

"Of the healing angels," she smiled.

"Oh," I said softly, for she amazed me by speaking of an area that was of great interest to me. "I would like that, but...," I grappled for the words as well as for direction, "I'm on my way to the throne room."

"This is on your way," she smiled. "Your heavenly Father is offering you this opportunity."[7]

I looked to Heather for guidance.

"I would go if I were you," she affirmed.

"Would you like to drop by?" Clara asked.[8]

"Yes," I said enthusiastically.

Clara laughed. "Thank you, Heather. She seems wonderfully refreshed."

"Yes, thank you, Heather," I added, turning to her, but

already she was fading into the mist of the waterfall, smiling and holding up her hand to acknowledge our departure as she disappeared.

We too left suddenly.

## The Annex

IMMEDIATELY WE WERE outside of a very large building that had a small sign over its double doors: THE ANNEX.[9] It was a short distance from an equally large building that had a sign written in a language that I could not read.

I thought to myself, *I wonder if travel is at the speed of thought here?*

We entered the building.

It was a huge auditorium much the same as the municipal auditoriums in major cities. There were a number of tiers, as well as the main floor. Angels filled the building. They all wore white armbands with a large red cross on each band.[10] They seemed to be attending a lecture.

Their instructor was on an elevated platform before a gigantic, clear board that looked similar to lucid plastic. He held a long pointer with which he would add colored-light illustrations to the board by touching it. He did not draw or write, but pointed only; they appeared on the board complete in their design.

Clara began to make her way to the front of the auditorium. The angels remained attentive, but they moved aside so that we could pass down the aisle. We stood near the raised platform, and I could see the instructor more clearly.

He had a crew cut and wore white armbands with a red cross on each band. He also had stripes on his sleeves.

## Angels of Healing

I TURNED TO look at the faces of the angels. They looked like the United Nations of angelhood, representing many nation-alities.[11] I supposed that the Lord would send them on assignments all over the world. They were very intent upon the lecture.

The instructor continued, "You realize that you play a very important role in verifying our Lord's victory in the area of health. The enemy will use any wile to attempt to bring into a place of unbelief those to whom our God assigns you. He is a master of unbelief. He has succeeded mightily with human-kind in general and with the elect specifically. It is often easier for the redeemed to believe our Lord will provide for them financially than to believe He wants His people well. The healing revival is about to begin.[12] Instead of one, we will be assigning two of you to each person slated for the gift of healing.[13]

"We want you to learn to work together now. We have some badges for you to fasten to those receiving this gift."

He held up a badge. It was green with red letters: ONLY BELIEVE.[14]

"We have a large number of the redeemed who will be here later, who will act like believers on earth.[15] Don't be discour-aged by what they say to you. They are here to show you exactly what you might be facing with your charges. Some of the replies they will give you will seem fantastic, but they are usual. You will be able to see how effectively the enemy has eroded belief in the Lord's gracious provision of health. Work through this dismay now. We've given you a 'buddy system' for this revival. There are to be many, many with the gift of healing this time around. Any questions?"

"When will this be?" an angel shouted from far back in the hall.

"The Lord God, the Almighty, knows this. You just get ready!" he called to the angel asking the question. "He did say, 'Soon'; I can tell you that much. That is the reason for this mobiliza-tion and intensification of training. Any other questions?"

There was general silence.

"All right, I want you to rally back here after your work with the redeemed. Do not, and let me repeat this, do *not* indi-vidually question the redeemed so that you 'bone up' before this workout. We want the full impact of their answers to hit you together. If there are no other questions, you are dismissed."

There was a great deal of movement as the angels rose and began talking to one another while leaving. Clara and I started up some stairs toward the top of the platform. The instructor was clearing the transparent board as we reached the top.

## The Angelic Instructor

"HELLO, CLARA. WHO is this with you?" he teased, as an adult might tease about a child whom he knows well.

"I believe you know Ann," Clara said, playing along.

His eyes twinkled. "Yes, I do know her. If I hadn't told the trainees to refrain from cramming for this exam, I could have had Ann give them some of the answers they will hear on earth."

"Now, Chabburah," Clara smiled, shaking her head as one might when indulging an inveterate jokester. I knew what he meant, however, so I changed the subject.

"What are the stripes on your sleeve?" I asked.

"By His stripes we are healed," he smiled tenderly, looking at the stripes.[16]

Clara continued: "We're taking a tour. Do you have any suggestions?"

"The hanging gardens..." he began.

"No," she laughed, "concerning the healing angels and the revival that is coming in the area of healing."

He looked at a slate in his hand with mock seriousness. "Well, I see here that Ann is slated for a couple of my finest angels."

"Me?" I questioned. "Is it possible?" I knew that God gave this giftedness to some of His children. In fact, I had stepped into a stream of such a gift at one time. It was as though God healed everyone for whom I prayed. This amazing and utterly supernatural anointing lasted for several months, and then it was gone.[17] Why He gave it and why the anointing lifted, I never understood. Since that time, there were more questions than answers in my mind.

# Angels in Training

## Classes

THE INSTRUCTOR DID not respond to my inner dialogue, but continued, "Clara, I would suggest that she begin classes soon. She's almost a classic example of 'gelatin belief'—'touch it and it shakes.' I'm going to teach these classes myself," he continued. "She can study this series at home as a correspondence course, but since she's here right now, she could tour the warehouse."

Clara turned to me. "Would you like that?"

"Yes," I said. "If the Lord is going to use me to pray for healing in others, I . . . well, I need to learn all that I can."

"All right," he said. "You can get a head start by touring next door; we'll page you when you're to begin your course at home. How's that?"

"That sounds good to us," Clara said, "We'll begin right away. Thank you." She began moving us toward the stairs of the platform.

"Yes, thank you," I said.

## The Request

HE CALLED AFTER us, "Now don't talk to any of the students on your way out. You might tempt one of them to stumble and ask you questions," he chuckled. Suddenly, as if struck by a thought, he called to us.

"Wait a minute. This is really an excellent opportunity. You're here, and . . . " I could not understand what he was saying. "Would you be willing for the students to question you in order that they might hear your reasoning?" he asked. "Sometimes it's difficult for the redeemed believers up here to remember why they thought as they thought while on earth. Would you be willing?"

"Mercy," I laughed lightly. "Am I so tough?"

"No, no, no," he said, putting down his slate and crossing to place his hands on my shoulders. "You're just . . . typical of the reasoning given on earth."

"If it would be helpful to you and the others..." I said.

"It would," he replied. "Good! You and Clara tour next door. We'll page you there," he said, going back to the large board. But almost immediately he whipped around again to look at us. "Now, don't ask Clara about healing," he smiled. "We want a raw example for them."

"Okay," I laughed.

He went back to his board, and we started down the stairs. Immediately we were at the back of the large auditorium and exiting the double doors.

As we stepped from the building, we could see thousands of angel trainees sitting on the lawn in twos with one or two of the redeemed. They were in deep discussions.

I looked up at the sign over the doorway of the building toward which we were walking. I could not read it before, but now, much to my amazement, it appeared clearly: BODY PARTS.

Clara opened the door, and we stepped inside.

# 4

# Healing Angels

T HE WAREHOUSE WAS large, as large as the auditorium we had just left and as white as a "clean room" at a research facility. It seemed unusually bright in the building, as though the contents were either preserved or incubated in light.

"This building holds an inventory of available parts of the human body," Clara said.[1]

There were bins upon bins of parts of all colors and sizes.

### The Warehouse Workers

ANGELS IN WHITE were working inside. These angels were the

size of humans and had no wings. Each wore an arm band with the same red cross on it. One of these angels walked over to us. "We're pleased that you have come to visit the parts department, Ann."

"How do you know me?" I asked.

"We know everyone slated for the gift of healing," he smiled. "You need to know that these are available."

He walked with us down the wide, center aisle. As I looked at the bins, I wondered what it might be like to have the gift of healing for the remainder of my life. Through the written Word, Jesus commands us to heal the sick and raise the dead, but I was not among those through whom He was fulfilling His own command consistently. Healing seemed as general a commission to Christians as "go ye...," but many of us saw little of the early church's power to heal physically. I had always made excuses for others and myself, but secretly, I wondered why.

The angel continued, "We're ready here. The Lord has made ample provision. Please enjoy your tour."

"We will," Clara said.

"Yes," I said, somewhat distractedly.

He bowed slightly from the waist and stepped backward before returning to his work.

## The Page

THERE WERE SO many questions I wanted to ask Clara. Suddenly a piece of paper floated before our eyes and paused in the air. It read, "Please return to the annex." Then it zipped away.

"This is sooner than I thought," Clara said.

We turned and began to walk toward the door of the warehouse. In hushed tones I said, "Oh, Clara, this is getting really exciting. I'm going to be able to help these angels. What an honor...what a gift!"

"Yes," she agreed.

"And just think, I might see some of these angels with other people during the revival," I mused.

We exited the warehouse and began to cross to the annex.

I was reiterating to myself, "...to assist angels." Then I addressed Clara again, "...because you angels are so helpful to us, but rarely do we get the opportunity to help you."

She gave a wise smile that seemed to indicate that this was not true but did not want to dampen my enthusiasm.

## Angels Who Have Their Stripes

WE ENTERED THE annex. Again a crowd of angels filled the room. A group of angels was on the platform. They wore no arm bands but had red stripes up and down the sleeves of their garments. We stood in the back of the hall.

"These are angels who have their stripes," Clara said. "The Lord assigned them to believers during the last healing revival."[2]

"There aren't many of them," I said.

Clara sighed, "No, only a few on earth were given the gift of healing in great measure. These believers were meant to train the many; instead, most of them erected tents and held the gift for themselves. The gift was used, but since they did not train others, it was corrupted and became a means of enriching themselves personally."

She glanced out over the large auditorium and smiled as she continued, "This roomful is only one group of trainees. Others are at other levels of training; some have their stripes already and are beginning to join those to whom the Lord assigned them. Many of the redeemed on earth have been taking a correspondence course, most without knowing it. The believer needs to complete the course before he receives the two assigned angels. So, everyone is in training right now, aren't they?"

"Is this correspondence course the same that I'll take?" I asked.

"Yes," she said. "It is study concerning healing in the Word."[3] She then turned her attention to the angels on the platform.

There was a great deal of light coming from these angels. One was speaking. "The Lord wishes those of us who were used in the last revival to hold a reunion on earth before the beginning of this outpouring of the Holy Spirit. You might say that we are bringing closure to that which was. We are being honored by the reunion being the commencement celebration that will usher in the next great move of our God for healing."

Another of the veteran angels interjected, "We know what your next question will be: 'When?'"

There was a chuckle of laughter from the trainees.

"We don't know when, but the Lord has said, 'Soon.'"

I whispered to Clara, "What beautiful angels."

"Yes," she said.

## The Former Outpouring

ANOTHER ANGEL ON the platform spoke. "That which occurred during the last great outpouring of the Spirit for healing was very painful to all of us." They shook their heads, sadly looking at one another.

"Corruption crept in," another said, "elusive sin by elusive sin. Finally, most had corrupted the gift beyond the recognition of those of us who were serving them."

"Mankind may be deceived by outward show," another angel said, "but we saw all that happened. God is not mocked."

They paused a moment; the gravity of that which had occurred was still painful to them.

The first angel spoke again. "In this coming revival the gift will be so widespread that the corruption due to pride and power is less likely to occur."

To his statement, another angel added, "But watch for these: pride, the lust for power, greed, and sexual lust."[4]

"It will not be the lesser demons you will need to battle, but demons as strong as you and rabidly determined because the time is short," the first angel said.[5] "We'll turn the meeting over to Chabburah again," he concluded.[6]

The angels seated in the auditorium stood before the angels on the platform and blew toward them.[7] I supposed that this was some form of a standing ovation.

"Thank you," they smiled.

Chabburah spoke to them briefly. Then they left the platform. Chabburah came to the center of the platform. "Remember, these friends will be available to answer questions and assist, not only now, but when the revival begins."

The other angels were touching the angels with stripes as the latter walked through the crowd. As they passed, they saw me and acknowledged Clara. The last angel stopped before me. "Hello, Ann," he said, touching my right shoulder. He looked into my eyes and then looked at Clara, smiled, and left.

"Stretch a bit," Chabburah said, "for Ann has come to be with us."

## Preparing to Teach

CLARA BEGAN TO move us to the front of the auditorium. The angels smiled as we passed. They were moving about and talking among themselves.

Chabburah was waiting for us on the platform, smiling, following us with his eyes. "There you are, Ann," he said effusively.

"This was very quick," Clara remarked.

"She was about to ask you questions," he shook his finger at me, as one would to tease a child. "Come over here," he added. "I have seats for you both. Sit down and make yourselves comfortable."

Then he turned to the auditorium. "All right, take your seats," he said to those who were talking. "You can talk later." He gestured toward me. "Ann is with us. She has graciously accepted an invitation to answer any questions you might have concerning her or humans in general."

I tugged at Chabburah's robe. "I don't know everything," I whispered to him.

Everyone laughed.

He smiled, "We know you don't know everything. We don't either, so we're all in good company. I'll just step back over here and let you begin."

## Teaching the Angels

I DID NOT know how I expected the meeting to be conducted, but I certainly did not expect to be handed "the floor." I was stiff as I began. "In the first place, it is such a blessing for me to be able to assist you. Hmmm…" I did not know where to start, so I just jumped in. "Well, most people on earth do not believe in divine healing."[8]

A mumble ran through the auditorium.

I continued, "Even those who are saved have a difficult time believing."

There was a very loud reaction. The amazement was such that I looked at Chabburah. He urged me to proceed.

"Even those who have seen divine healing have difficulty believing all the time."

There was general, loud alarm throughout the auditorium.

"Hold it down," Chabburah said. Then to me he said, "Why don't you suggest that they ask you questions?"

"Would you like to ask questions?" I asked rather meekly.

## Angelic Questions

AN ANGEL ROSE from his seat and spoke loudly, "Don't they believe the Word?"

"The unbelievers don't, of course. Some believers do, but many believers really do not."

There was a stunned silence in the auditorium. I looked at Chabburah. "Give them time, Ann," he said. "They're shocked."

"Some believers, you see, think that parts of the Bible do not apply today, that certain sections were for long ago," I said.

An angel near the platform said in a normal voice that carried because of the silence, "But the Word says that The Eternal is the same yesterday, today, and forever. Why would they consider the Word apart from Him? He is the Word."

There was a great deal of general agreement among the angels.

"Well," I shrugged and laughed, "they do."

"Do you?" another asked.

"I believe in healing, and I believe that the Lord promises health and that He has paid for healing for believers, but I do not understand it."

"It is a covenant promise," another angel said, rising from his seat.[9] "By His stripes He has knit you back or mended or joined you again to Him who is divine health. It is sure."

"But often people are sick," I said.

Another angel rose. "It's a covenant promise, as has been said. One needs to abide in Christ."

"Of course, if a person deliberately abuses his earthly vessel...," another said.

"Forgiveness needs to be absolute," another added without standing. "Break the knitting together with Christ, and some sort of illness will result."[10]

"As night follows day," they all said. You could tell they were members of a class. They all laughed.

I interjected, "But most who will receive this gift will not be abiding by the covenantal agreements won by Jesus. How can this be?"

### Grace

AGAIN THEY ALL laughed, responding in unison, "Grace."

Chabburah explained, "There is coming an outpouring of grace as the Holy Spirit moves in power in the coming revival." As he spoke to me, he added, "Are you tiring, Ann?"

"Yes, this is all so much," I chuckled wistfully.

"Students," Chabburah said, "that is enough for today. Let's stand and give Ann a big hand." The angels stood and cheered as they clapped. "All right, all right," he said, "settle down. You're dismissed." He turned to me, "Thank you, Ann. That was wonderful. These students thought they could not be shocked again."

"Why didn't they blow toward me as they did toward the angels who were here before me?" I asked.

He gave a mighty laugh. "It might have killed you," he said.

"They were passing the breath of God to them. That's the highest compliment they could pay the angels who were lecturing. The angels, being spirit as they are, could receive it. They breathed it in. The breath was as food to them. Although you are in spirit here, some experiences would be beyond your capacity at present."

He put one hand behind Clara and one hand behind me as we started down the steps to leave. I could tell that he was strengthening me as we walked. At the bottom of the steps stood two blond, rather nervous-looking angels.

## The Twins

"CHABBURAH," ONE SAID, "we'd like to meet Ann."

"Of course," he said with great understanding, almost tenderly. "Ann, these are the angels whom the Lord has assigned to you for the revival."

These angels looked seven feet tall, young, eighteen to twenty years old; they appeared identical. "You look like twins," I said.

"Yes," the other said, "I'm Rapha, and he's Raphashanah."[11]

Raphashanah said, "Thank you for sharing with us. We need as much understanding as possible before we are on the job."

"Thank you for saying that," I said. "I became tired, and Chabburah felt that was enough."

"It was most helpful," said Rapha.

"I'll be taking classes; maybe we could talk more then," I added.

They looked at Chabburah. He nodded yes. "Yes," they smiled broadly, "we'll talk more then."

"You students are going to miss your next class if you don't hurry," Chabburah said to them.

"Very well," they smiled, "we'll see you later," and ran off.

"I'm staying here, Clara," Chabburah said. "And thank you, Ann. That was most helpful. Now, don't forget, we'll send a page to you when class is to begin."

"I'll be ready," I said as I hugged him. I had never hugged

an angel. They do not feel exactly the same as flesh and blood on earth. Not as solid, I suppose is the best way to express it, but substantial.[12]

"See you later, Clara," he said.

"Yes," she replied.

"Good-bye," we both said, and we started to walk away from the platform. Suddenly we were at the back of the auditorium and exiting the doors. By stepping onto the path, we were quickly quite a distance from the two buildings.

## *He Comes*

IMMEDIATELY AHEAD OF us on the path was a burning light. Hundreds of spirits surrounded this brilliance, darting in and lifting out like eagles catching heat currents. They were flying with the light as if escorting it. So bright was this great light that it reduced the spirits to silver outlines of themselves in its radiance. It reminded me of figures passing in front of bright headlights on a dark night, although here there was no surrounding darkness. Everything paled that was near this intense brightness.

Clara spoke to me. "He is coming," she said. "He comes for you, Ann."

Both of our faces were catching the glow of His radiance. My heart leaped within me, yet a peace settled over me like warm oil.

Clara continued, "We will be with one another later. All of your attention needs to be given to Him now." She smiled toward the light and vanished.

# 5

## The Lord Jesus

H E WAS COMING—my Beloved, my Friend.
My breath was knocked out of me, and my knees went slack as He came closer. Then, like a tree overtaken by a dust cloud from a wind flurry, the cloud of His glory engulfed me. The spirits still were darting in and lifting out on the periphery, but I could see only Him.

### Remembering

I HAD SEEN Him standing in the sanctuary of a church several times before over a period of years. The last time was two and a half months earlier. He was standing twenty-four feet high in the sanctuary of a church where the pastors met for citywide prayer meetings. It was Yom Kippur. For four years we had labored in the citywide prayer movement of that metropolitan area, and we had returned to the city for a Bible conference after being gone for a year.

At that time He stood in the sanctuary, a rainbow encircling Him, clothed in a shimmering, multicolored cloak.[1] The light radiating from Him looked alive. Suddenly He telescoped to the size of a man and spoke.

"Look at Me," He said. His eyes, though far away, suddenly were near and riveting, as if aflame.

As I looked into His eyes, the robe of vibrating colors passed through His body, came to me, and encircled my body. I could feel it as well as see it.

Then, without walking, He came forward until He passed right into my body.[2] He was facing the back of my head, and I was facing the back of His.[3] He turned around within my body, and we were both facing in the same direction, both wearing the cloak. After this I had the even stranger sensation of having someone look out of my eyes—Jesus, not I, was looking out of my eye sockets.[4]

Suddenly He moved forward out of my body, leaving the cloak on me and returning to the place from which He had come. In an instant He disappeared, and I was left wearing the shimmering, multicolored cloak.[5]

The experience two and a half months before this present moment when He stood before me in heaven seemed wonderfully strange and yet very natural. But I had never understood what it all meant. I expected some change in my life, some increased anointing, but I found myself amazingly the same and stunningly unanointed, which was usual.

## The Desire of All Nations

Now He was standing before me in Paradise.

How can one describe "the Desire of All Nations"? Far more

than the impact of His physical appearance, He embodies life. His eyes are clear blue but as deep as a bottomless pool. It seems that if you could travel into those eyes, you would understand all mysteries, that in plunging toward the bottom of that deep pool, you would pass the answers to all things.

He embodies love, light, and truth. A kaleidoscope of understandings flooded my spirit, computing faster than lightning, causing me to react as Job reacted when the Lord confronted him—I could only cover my mouth.[6]

He stepped up to me.

He was smiling broadly, as a childhood sweetheart that you knew you would always, always love, but that you had not seen since childhood. The years dropped away as you saw Him, and you were right—you would always, always love Him; no one could ever take His place.

He took my right hand in His left, which strengthened me.

"Come," He said. Immediately we were flying.[7]

## The Mountains of Spices

PARADISE BEGAN TO pass beneath us. The spirits accompanying Him flew to the side and behind us. We were flying up to an astonishing mountain range. The color of each mountain varied. As we drew closer, I realized that the first mountain emitted an aroma.

"Where are we, Lord?" I asked.

"You have often called Me to the mountains of spices," He said.[8] "We are here."

Aromatic spices were growing on these mountains. The colors, as well as the aromas, varied from mountain to mountain.

## The Father's Delight

"THESE ARE FOR your Father's delight," Jesus said, "and for the delight of His children. They bring joy." Without turning His head to look at me, He asked, "Do you wish to bring joy?"

"Yes," I answered.

Jesus responded, "Obedience brings joy to My Father, holiness of heart, thankfulness, truth with mercy. Each is like a spice. Each has a fragrance. Collectively the aromas are pleasing to My Father. The aromas speak of Me to Him, not just one spice but the aroma of the blend as one passes from mountain to mountain. Together they witness of Me, and this pleases My Father. Also the aroma of these spices coming from His adopted children speaks of Me, and He is pleased."

As we passed over each mountain, wave upon wave of the most tantalizingly delicious smells washed over me. Then some of the particular spices growing from each flew up into my free arm and hand. As we passed over the twelfth mountain, my arm and hand were full of the complete complement of aromatic spices from the mountain range; the smell was beyond compare. I breathed in deeply and felt permeated with the aroma. I could almost taste the fragrance.

Suddenly I wanted to give out that which had come to me. I flung the spices up into the air, and they became white doves.

"My covenant of peace," Jesus said.[9]

Before my eyes I could see the whole earth as if I were the distance of a satellite from it. The doves flew and became flames of fire resting over the whole earth.[10]

The picture before my eyes so intrigued me that I did not realize that the spirits had disappeared and that Jesus and I were coming down into a walled garden.

## The Walled Garden

THE ENCLOSURE SEEMED to be a private garden.[11] It was not extremely large, but it was large enough to have a variety of trees as a part of its planting: the pomegranate, myrtle, and cedar; the balsam, cinnamon, frankincense, myrrh, and aloe.

The garden was in the full bloom of spring with narcissus and jonquils in the beds and vines of yellow jasmine and purple wisteria intertwined on the stone wall.

There was a three-tiered fountain in the center of the garden with a bench near it. The bench was under a very large apricot tree, which resembled more an oak than a fruit tree. It was in bloom also and exuded a lovely, invigorating scent.

Our feet came to rest on the ground near the fountain.

"What a lovely garden," I said.

"Yes," He smiled, allowing His eyes to scan the area lightly. "I enjoy walking here."

Suddenly into my mind came a phrase from the Song of Solomon: "Until the cool of the day when the shadows flee away..."[12] It was cool here, and certainly there were no shadows. Did that song speak of Paradise?

We began to walk.

## A Garden for Lovers

THE PATH CIRCLED the garden, with plantings and beds near the wall as well as on the opposite side of the path in the center of the garden. Camphire (henna) was blooming there, and the star-of-Bethlehem, blue flax, and the scarlet lily were blooming in beds near it.

"Who tends this garden?" I asked.

"You do," He answered.

"I tend this garden?" I exclaimed with astonishment.

"Yes," He replied.

I looked over the garden. I felt that I had been here before, but the feeling was an elusive impression, rather like trying to piece together a dream when you only remember snatches of it. I could not bring it into clear focus.

"Would You tell me of this garden, Lord?" I asked finally.

"Each such garden is different. Each is unique, and I delight in each." He paused before speaking again. "Do you enjoy being here?" He asked.

"Yes, it's..." I could not find the words.

"Yes," He agreed.

We came to a spring that flowed from a rock in the garden. Spanning the water was an arch of a bridge that seemed only wide enough for two people. As I thought about it, the bench near the fountain also seemed only wide enough to seat two. Perhaps this was a garden for lovers. As we crossed the bridge, I could smell the scented calamus that grew on the banks by the water.

## *His Burden*

"DO YOU BECOME tired?" I asked.

"There is a burden in My heart for mankind," He replied. "I will bear this burden until all is completed, but this is not like the body fatiguing and needing rest.[13] No, I do not tire as those who are housed in the flesh tire."

"Do You get lonely?" I asked.

"I long for completion, but that is not loneliness.[14] Loneliness comes from unfulfilled desires, passions that cause one to seek to live in the future through a desire for fulfillment. I live in the present. I am concerned with that which is now. All things are complete here...although incomplete moment by moment. I long for the completion of this gift to My Father, that He may be glorified as well as pleased.[15] He loves having His children around Him. What satisfaction is greater: a crown upon the head, a smile in the heart, a joy that is beyond compare."

We passed beds of saffron and nard. I remembered that on earth these were of great worth.

He continued, "The eyes of those in Satan's kingdom are blind to My Father, as well as to Me, but they are open to and aware of their subsistence coming from the evil one. He too has gifts, and he displays them. The harlot stands in the doorway and beckons the naive: 'Come in; my bed is scented with all manner of spices and balms. Your sleep will be sweet.'

"But it will not be sweet. A thousand torments embrace the one on that bed; a thousand heartaches that can never be satisfied lie with the naive on that bed. True love springs forth from God, a never-ceasing fountain fed by springs of living water within the Godhead.[16] I am that Spring. I am that Fountain. I AM."

By now we had circled half of the garden and were back at the center fountain. We sat on the bench.

"Lord," I said, "show me something precious in Your sight."

He opened His hand, and in it was a tear. "In this tear is a world, a universe, an infinity of love. In this tear is the DNA, as it were, of a loved one's spiritual genes. In this tear are salt and light. I can look into this tear and see the face of God, for it is clear. I can look through it to Him who births the universe. This tear is very precious to Me."[17]

We both looked at the tear, and then He closed His hand and continued, "Close your eyes and hold out your hand."

I closed my eyes, and He placed into my hand something smooth.

"Now open your eyes."

## A New Name

I OPENED MY eyes and my right hand to look at a smooth, white stone with the name *Anna* engraved upon it.

"Your new name," He said.[18] "I am adding the breath of life to your name. Here you will be called Anna."

"Anna," I said to myself.

"Now, Anna, My sister and My love, our names have been joined in covenant."

"Thank You," I said, holding the stone to my heart.

"I have been waiting for you, Anna. The loneliness you experienced is nothing compared to the heartache I experienced as I waited for you, seeing you run after all manner of idols to seek satisfaction." He looked out into the garden. "How I called to you."[19] There was pain in His voice. "Year after year you dallied, and I grieved, waiting for you to realize that no one can, nor ever will, bring you life itself but Me alone."

His words struck me to the heart. "My Lord and my God," I said quietly, "no one has ever loved me as You have..." I was choked with emotion. Slowly I continued, "Nor ever desired my company as...," but I could not finish.

"None of flesh and blood can, Anna, for you belong to Me."

He looked me in the eye, and His eyes pierced through me. "I created you for Myself, and only I can satisfy you truly and fully."

## A Gift to God

I DID NOT know what to say. I searched, trying to think of some reply. Finally I asked, "If I am created for You, Lord, what can I do for You? How...," I groped for the words to convey that I wanted to give a gift to Him. "How do I give something to You?"

He searched my face for a moment and then smiled. "Sing for Me, Anna; that would comfort Me." He leaned back against the large, apricot tree and closed His eyes.

I did not know what to sing. I swallowed hard. Then I looked out over the garden and prayed within myself. Soon, without knowing what I would say, I began to sing:

> Where golden light becomes the red,
> And red becomes the white,
> Burning with the zeal of love,
> A land devoid of night,
> Powering the universe
> From star to distant star;
> Consume the dross, O Ancient One,
> Let no aberrance mar
> All that belongs to You alone,
> Created by Your word;
> All that is seen and understood,
> All hidden and unheard.
> Consume the sin, O Ancient One,
> Consign it to the night;
> For us there's oneness with our God,
> The Everlasting Light.
> No shadow dare exalt itself,
> No darkness dare display,
> Where God Eternal rules and reigns
> The land of endless day.

Praise Him, all you heavenly host,
Praise Him, sons of men.
Turn your faces toward the Son,
God's "Yea" and His "Amen."

I had never heard that song before. At its completion I sat amazed. My right hand came up to cover my mouth.

## That Which Is Coming

THERE WAS A long pause after the song ended. Finally He spoke, "Before the cock crows, Anna, three stages of betrayal will have been accomplished against Me in the world. Betrayal is multiplying, and many will be seduced by their own fear and need for survival.[20] They will betray to save themselves."

"Lord, unless You give us the grace, we will all betray You. Who is strong enough to think he can stand? You must strengthen us. Unless You rise up to pass these tests...," I was momentarily speechless at the thought, "...who would not, for the slightest reason, betray You? Help us! Rise up within us, Lord. Do not let us sin against You."

He opened His eyes and turned His head to look at me. "I have heard this, Anna." He continued to look at me silently, as if meditating upon my features. Then He sat up straight and said, "Walk with Me to the gate." He rose from the bench and helped me to stand also. We walked silently to the golden filigree gate. The two doors of the gate opened as we approached. We walked out, and He closed the gates, looking into the quiet garden within the wall.

"It is very beautiful here," I said, also looking back at the garden.

## The Golden Key

JESUS TURNED AND handed me a golden key to the gate's lock. "Here is the key," He said. "Go in whenever you like." The key was large and antique in design. It hung on a red cord. "Here,"

He continued, and He dropped the cord with the key on it over my head.

"Will You meet me here?" I asked.

"Unlock the gate, and I will meet you here," He smiled.

I looked again at the garden.

"Whenever you wish," He repeated, "meet Me here." And then He disappeared.

I looked down at the white stone in my hand and the golden key resting on the area of my heart.

It was then that I heard the sound of singing, faintly at first. It was the sort of singing you might hear if your mother was making bread in the kitchen on a cold winter's day. I turned toward the sound and saw a bright light. In the center of this light sat a group of spirits.

The path lay right near them. I stepped onto the path to approach them.

## 6

~⚬~

# The Eagle's Nest

THE LIGHT WAS as white and intense as the "incubating" light in the parts department. Within the light, four spirits sat together working. Intermittently each would reach up and take a blue ribbon from the air as it floated into the light. The ribbons also seemed charged with light as the spirits began to roll them onto large, silver spools. Then, with the ribbons wrapped, they would place the spools onto equally large, silver spindles that were suspended in midair.

# The Eagle's Nest

## Spirits of the Spools and Spindles

THESE SPIRITS WERE not solid in appearance. They were closer to being transparent, but a bluish-silver light outlined their forms. Their shape was that of human beings. However, the light in which they worked made it difficult to see their facial features distinctly.

They did not seem to notice me as they sang together while they worked:

> Every little seam,
> Every little seam
> Sewn with the thread of life;
> Every little seam
> Joins the living stream
> Flowing to the river of life.

Then, without turning, they acknowledged me. "Hello, Anna," a spirit spoke from all that light. "Watching?"

"Yes," I said.

"We are getting the ribbons together for sewing. They represent the various streams that flow from the great river of life and back into it, even as the waters on earth flow in and out but do not overwhelm the land."[1]

"These streams are God's people," another spirit said.[2] "They come from Him and flow back to Him, the great Source."

"But they need to be sewn together," another said, looking toward me as if suggesting my participation.

"I'm not a very good seamstress," I laughed lightly.

"The needle here is the sword not of man.[3] The streams are being sewn together by the Spirit of God Himself so that the Father might rejoice to see His city filled with those who love His Son and one another. Even the city itself is made glad."[4]

"You are called to sew with such a needle, Anna," the first spirit said. "That we do know."

"We are placing the spools of ribbon on spindles so that

they will unravel easily when ready to be brought together," the fourth spirit added.

"Is there some significance to placing them on spindles?" I asked.

### Oil From Heaven

THE SPIRITS SMILED at one another and sang:

> There is oil in the spindles,
> Oil right from God.
> There is oil from the Spirit of God.
> There is oil like a gusher,
> Oil from the sky,
> Oil that's been hidden until now.[5]
> Hum-hum, oil from on high,
> Oil that's been hidden until now.
> Hum-hum, oil of the Spirit,
> Oil that's been hidden until now.

One of the spirits turned to me and said, "These ribbons are being placed on spindles for you and others who will use the sword as a needle to prepare for the gusher."

Then they sang:

> Sew the streams together
> And catch the sacred oil;
> And, oh, let it not be
> Used for the profane.

"Your Father has the answers to the questions in your heart," the third spirit smiled. "We are those who wrap the spools and put them onto the spindles."

### Ribbons of Blue

"THEY ARE ALL blue ribbons," I said.

"Yes, each became a stream when revelation came concerning a great truth about our God. But a truth *about* Him is not Him," the first spirit added. "Although the ribbons are being wrapped on individual spools, they are about to be sewn together into a river like the river of life from which they came."

"As we see the Lord bringing into completion all things relating to these times and seasons, we rejoice to be a part of His great roundup," the second spirit smiled.

## The White Eagle

SUDDENLY THE WINGS of a large bird passed over me.

The spirits to whom I was speaking looked up and rose to their feet immediately. I too looked up and saw a large, totally white Eagle. He was powerful, fierce, and majestic in flight. I had never heard of a completely white eagle.

"Stretch out your hands," He said as He began His descent.

The spirits bowed toward the Eagle. I did not know what to do but to stretch out my hands. The Eagle, as large as I, backed into me so that His eyes and beak were where my face was. Then just as quickly He was before me again, with His eyes piercing into mine.

I gasped.

Just as quickly, the Eagle changed into the Lord. He said, "This is so you may know that 'the testimony of Jesus is the spirit of prophecy.'" Then He became the white Eagle again.[6] "Come," He said.

I put my arms around His neck, and we flew upward. I did not even think to say good-bye to the spirits who were wrapping the spools. As I lay down with my arms around His neck and my head near the back of His head, I could feel the motion of flying beneath me. His feathers were snowy, and His scent made me want to bury my face deep within His feathers. Beneath the white feathers the great Eagle's skin looked like pure gold.

### His Nest

WE CAME QUICKLY to an outcropping of rock near the top of a mountain. An eagle's nest was positioned on this rocky thrust.[7] The nest was large, perhaps five feet across, and made of strong tree branches. I climbed from His back and stepped down onto small, downy feathers within the nest. The white Eagle perched on the nest's rim.

We were on earth.

The view of the circling mountain range and valley below was breathtaking, but I did not know where we were. The air was clean there, and the view from such a high ledge was sweeping in its expanse. The mountains and the valleys were lush and green. There were passing clouds and shadows from the slant of the sun. Beautiful—but it was not Paradise.

As I viewed the surrounding mountain range, a string of very large paper dolls floated by.

The great Eagle spoke, "So much of what is happening now in the body of Christ is like paper dolls—one copying the other."[8]

The paper dolls disappeared, and an eagle of pure gold flew by. "I am looking for an eagle of gold, Anna—rare beyond measure." As He spoke, power like a surge of electricity ran all over the eagle of gold. It became pure white, like the great white Eagle. "The golden eagle becomes like Me," He said.[9]

Then a line of large, paper, cut-out eagles floated across the mountain range. They were hooked together as the floating paper dolls had been.

### The White Eagle's Invitation

HE CONTINUED, "THERE are many eagles, for I am generous with the gift of the Holy Spirit.[10] But, Anna, I am giving you an invitation to become an eagle of gold."

Suddenly I saw a rocket blast off from the earth and shoot into heaven. The great Eagle continued, "The golden eagle's nest is in heaven. The golden eagle does not even eat earthly food. It feeds above. The paper doll eagles catch fish, kill snakes, chase rabbits; but the eagle of gold breathes the ether above. It does not seek after or eat carrion. The golden eagle eats from the hand of God until it looks and smells and is like Me—pure white. There are many that *look* like Me, but you must eat from the hand of God to *be* like Me."

His eyes were aflame now. "Will you fly with Me, Anna, over streets of gold? Will you fly with Me over lakes so clear that the bottom is as the top? Leave the snakes, the bugs, the rabbits running rabbit trails. Come with Me and feed from the hand of God."

I paused to consider my answer—and He was gone.[11]

## Back in Paradise

I FOUND MYSELF back in Paradise, seated alone on a high hill.

Did I pause too long to contemplate, weighing His passion against my inertia? Was I fearful? Of what? What kept me from leaping up in my spirit and shouting, "Yes! I accept the invitation! Take me to Your resting place above and make of me an eagle of gold. I want to eat from the hand of God. I yearn for the intimacy You are offering." Why did I hesitate?

Now from that place of solitude on the hill in Paradise, my heart cried out, "O God, I long for You alone. Do what You will with me, for I am Yours. Yours alone! Yours alone!" There was such longing in my heart's cry that I expected to see Him charging over the hilltop on a white horse in response, but He did not.

Instead, silence.

## Passing Praise

THEN, ALMOST IMPERCEPTIBLY at first, I heard voices in the distance singing praises to God. The music came closer, but I could see no one. Instruments joined the song that now sounded as if it were being sung by a multitude of voices. The praise was rolling along like a flash flood in a wadi. Although

I could see no one, the praise seemed to be passing before me on this hill and moving in the direction of the path below. My ears caught the words of the singing:

> Let my life extol the living God,
> The Father of all light.
> From the ends of the earth through the universe,
> Extol His mercy and might.
> Forever is not long enough
> To praise His glorious name,
> The forever of forever
> To shout His glory and fame.
> O celestial court, throw down your crowns
> 'Neath the ruler of the earth.
> Living creatures, sing your songs
> To the King of the universe.
> O joy unspeakable, joy foretold,
> Ever new and ever old,
> Before the Father's throne be bold
> To lift your songs of praise.

Then I saw one angel after another join themselves to this praise, seemingly riding along on it. They would rise when the music would rise, and sank down when the music lowered, like the tail of a kite. Evidently they could see the praise, although I could not, because they looked as though they were touching it and being carried along.

Then, from near me on the hill, came the clear, pure sound of a flute. I turned to see an exquisite angel dressed in green playing the instrument. Her eyes were closed in worship, and I knew that the music she was playing was joining the praise passing before my eyes.

# 7

# Obedience

HE ANGEL SAT cross-legged on the ground playing a golden flute. Her hair was a rich auburn and plaited into seven large loops that were interlaced with gold. She wore a gossamer, green under tunic bound with a golden girdle, and a cloak with long sleeves, which was also green.

Within the sleeves of the outer garment were oversized pockets containing all manner of instruments used in the arts—all of gold.[1] There were various musical instruments, paint brushes, musical scores, ballet shoes, a quill pen—all within the sleeves. Her neck and hands had a slight tint of gold and so did the small portion of her bare feet that I could see.[2]

Secured around her head was a golden cord; in the center of the cord was a small golden box. The box was in the middle of her forehead and similar to a frontlet for the housing of Scripture.[3]

Eventually she lowered the flute and opened her eyes peacefully, as one might who is still rapt in contemplation. Then turning her face toward me, she smiled. "Praise Him," she said. Her voice was gentle and melodious, and her eyes a limpid green.

I was too disquieted in spirit to share her peace, for thoughts were racing through my mind—with no resolution.

## The Angel Judy

SHE SMILED AGAIN, knowingly this time, but did not address my private conflict. "I am Judy," she said, "one who praises."

"Hello, Judy," I said without much enthusiasm, "I am Anna."

"I know who you are," she smiled, "for I am assigned to you to assist you in praise of our God."[4]

"Assigned to me for praise?" I asked. Then excitedly I gestured toward the space in midair, "I saw . . ."

"Yes," she said, "angels traveling on praise."[5]

"Traveling on praise?"

"Yes," she reiterated, placing the flute into one of her oversized pockets.

"I do not understand."

"Praise has in it part of the heart and part of the spirit sent forth, and so it is tangible to us in this world of true light, life, and spirit. To us here, praise is as substantive as a trolley on earth, you might say. You join yourself to it, and it will carry you along. It can take you for a ride," she laughed liltingly, "and the one joined to it adds to it."

I turned my eyes to look out over the valley. *How could this be?* I questioned within myself. Then I began to think, *Yes, yes, I can understand that. I know that if someone leads worship with an anointing on earth, it can lift you in spirit to that person's level of praise. The other's anointing carries you with it, and you add your voice to the worship being raised to God. Yes, I can see that.*

"Since all such praise travels to the Father," she continued, "it is like catching a ride on a passing trolley and enjoying the ride to the throne room. If the angels do not ride all the way there, still they have added an imprint to the praise. Therefore, they too have participated, if ever so briefly."

The sound of a single violin began to pass by. The violin was playing a tender, unaccompanied melody. A single angel was traveling with the adoration being expressed through this instrument and was adding to it.[6]

"Some praise on earth is like a quiet stream, as is this," she smiled.

From a distance I could hear the sound of many voices singing. The sound was moving swiftly in our direction.

"Some worship is like a tidal wave," she said. "All of it gives to the angels a joy they would not have if mankind did not lift up praises to God."[7]

The sound was coming more quickly now, rolling toward us. As it drew nearer, I could sense my spirit rising to join such exalted worship. It lifted us spontaneously to our feet. Judy raised her hands, tilted her head back, and joined the song:

> Angels in their glory
> Can never touch the flame,
> The fire, pure incandescence,
> That burns within Your name.
> Let them gaze in wonder,
> In awe, as they proclaim:
> "Holy God, though ever new,
> Eternally the same."
>
> Frightened, frozen, fettered,
> Those who seek to fight,
> Numbed and gnawed and naked,
> Those who choose the night.

But we are covered by His love,
Beneath His banner stand,
Hidden in the Rock above,
Sheltered by His hand.

Angels in their glory
Can never touch the flame,
The fire, pure incandescence,
That burns within Your name.
Let them gaze in wonder,
In awe, as they proclaim:
"Holy God, though ever new,
Eternally the same."

In an ecstasy of devotion, Judy rose into the air from her place on the hill and began to move toward the passing praise.

"Take the path to find the Lord," she called, and she was swept along in the tidal wave of worship surging toward the throne.

The disappearing praise continued to engage my spirit. Finally I opened my eyes and realized that she had given me the answer I needed. I hurried down the hill to the path and began running in the direction of the vanishing praise.

## Obedience

AS I HASTENED, I heard the voice of Jesus say very clearly, "Obedience, Anna."

I stopped in my tracks.

He continued, "I delight to show you your heavenly home, but for your safety, you must be trained in obedience.[8] There are grave dangers.[9] All doors to the enemy must be shut."

As I stood in wonder at the gravity of what He had said, an angel appeared on the path beside me.

The angel began talking to me as though he were continuing some conversation we had already begun, gesturing with his hand toward God's park. "All of this is for the children of

God, but you, Anna, have chosen to eat from the hand of God. You must love your Father enough to choose obedience rather than gratifications on earth.[10] Choose Him minute by minute. You are careless with His gifts, and you are careless with His love for you."

His overfamiliarity stunned me, as well as his knowledge of a decision I had only recently made; but yes, I was careless. As the Lord had drawn me into a deeper walk with Him, those things permissible a year or even a month ago were now no longer allowable. Somehow I could no longer get by with them, but I still lapsed into many of these faults.

## The Thought Life

ELUSIVE SINS CAUSED me to pay a high price in my relationship with the Lord. I thought to myself, *Let the wicked forsake his way and the unrighteous man his thoughts.*[11] I had moved from the "way" category to the "thoughts." My mind did not focus on unforgiveness or covetousness or such obvious sins. My sins now were in engaging my mind in some area where I was not called, or in letting my mind dwell on the past, or in making a judgment that was out of my boundary of responsibility.

My life had become very constrained indeed.[12] If I walked without turning to the right or the left, I remained in the flow of God's grace. Any thoughts that were "vain in their imaginations" caused my mind to run in grooves around a track.[13] Such thoughts were driven by tormentors it seemed.[14] But I found that I could stop them by repeatedly catching myself and halting the train of thought as I began to think on such vain thoughts.

Of course, these thoughts would tiptoe back in, needing to be run out time and time again. Therefore I was halting them and throwing them out, standing against them with my will, as if my shoulder were against the door of access.

Still I was careless, as he had said, and was mentally running around many tracks in torment and weariness until each thought was taken captive to Christ.[15] Earlier in my life with Christ, my mind could usually do as it pleased, but not now.[16] Narrow and narrower was the way, but in this obedience to His Word was life.

## The Angel Shama

WITHOUT MISSING A beat, the angel on the path beside me said, "I am Shama."[17]

I saw no reason to give my name, for he seemed to know almost as much about me as I did myself.

"Shall we walk?" he continued.

Almost stumbling, I moved forward.

He had long, straight, silver hair that was caught at the base of his head and hung down his back. He was very muscular, and although his hair was silver, he looked perhaps forty. He wore a full-length white robe, which looked as though it had been stained with blood or the juice of red grapes. This stain was on the hem of the robe and on the cuffs of the long sleeves, discoloring the garment to the knees and elbows.

"You delight in God," he continued. "I have watched you and have seen that you desire nearness to Him. However, do you not know that disobedience creates a wall between you and Him?[18] It is a wall of your own making because you cannot curb your natural desires. He will replace with Himself every delight you push away, Anna."[19] In looking at me, his eyes caught sight of a hill slightly beyond us. "Come with me," he said.

As we walked up the hill, he continued, "There is a type of suffering in obedience, but the rewards far, far outweigh the pain."[20]

## The Prototypes Above

FROM THE TOP of the hill, we could see a broad plain below. Herds of various kinds of creatures were grazing; among them were prehistoric animals.[21]

My hands went to my face in amazement.

"Heaven itself is like an ark, Anna," he said. "These animals do not have resurrected bodies but were part of the heavenly kingdom before the earth was created."

"Magnificent," I whispered.

"Aren't they?" he said, observing the scene. Then, almost with a sigh, he continued, "Let's return to the path." He was slightly ahead of me going down the hill, and he assisted me with the incline.

"Do you have hair?" I asked him.

"It looks like hair," he said. "We are creatures of light. We are spirit, Anna. We are not flesh and blood as humans are. Some of us in service to the King look like humans, but some do not."[22]

We returned to the path and continued to walk. "We can change our appearance," the angel said, "whereas you cannot. We are known by the essence of what we are, not by our outward appearance. On earth this is often reversed, is it not? Humans often dwell upon appearances."

"You seem to know me," I queried.

"I know you better than you know me," the angel laughed.

## The Stained Robe

"WHY IS YOUR robe stained at the bottom and on the sleeves?"

"I am called to assist in child training—the kind that squeezes the child—like being in a wine press.[23] These," he looked down at the stains, "are visible signs of the child's development. The more stains, the greater the work has progressed within the child. Obedience is not learned easily, Anna. Some on earth never learn it."

"Are you an angel assigned to help train me?" I asked.

"I am assigned to you."

"Helping to train people in obedience cannot be a pleasant job."

The angel replied, "It is of great significance to the Father and absolutely necessary. By this time in your life, my robe should be entirely stained and my face and hands dripping, but there are only stains on the hem and sleeves. So may I suggest that you are hindering your growth through known disobedience. Immediate gratification can never replace serving the Lord with a whole heart. Such obedience releases joys untold."

## Repentance

I LOOKED OUT over the landscape, letting the truths he was sharing work within me. "I have sinned," I said quietly.[24] I did not wish to seem glib, but I did wish to show a willingness to repent promptly. "I ask the Lord to forgive me."

He put his arm around my shoulder and jostled me, as a coach might a football player. "And you know He does. This is a good day for new beginnings," he smiled. Then he removed his arm and looked ahead solemnly.

"I thank you for your patience and for helping me. I can see you are a powerful angel. If you were a human, I would say you 'worked out.'"

"We do 'work out,'" he laughed heartily, "but our workout comes from wrestling with humans.[25] I look as I do because you have given me so much resistance through your flesh. So," he laughed, "you might say I do 'work out.' I would suggest that you turn this very day so that my workout is less strenuous. Delight yourself in God, Anna, and reduce my exercise program," he smiled.

Then he sobered rapidly. "Nothing, no one can compare to Him," he said. "Speaking for those of us who are assigned to you," he continued haltingly, almost as if he was going to reveal something deeply personal, "we would like to get a little closer to God." He almost stammered, "If it were only us, we would; but much depends upon you concerning that."[26] He seemed so embarrassed by what he had said that he vanished.

# Obedience

## The Eagle Returns

BEFORE I COULD puzzle over what he meant, I saw the white Eagle fly across the path. My heart leaped when I saw Him. I began to run after Him, calling, "Lord! Lord, please come back, please."

He must have heard me, for He made a wide bank in flight and landed before me. I was so overjoyed to see Him whom my heart adores that I hugged Him around the neck, clinging to Him. "I want to fly with You. I want to eat from the hand of God."

He became the Lord. I buried my face in His shoulder. He held me, returning my embrace, more like a lover than a friend.[27] This amazed me. Did He long for me as I longed for Him?

"Forgive me, Lord," I said. "I want to be with You. I long for You. I want to be and do whatever You want, as long as we are together."

"Anna," He said, pulling me away from Him so that He could look into my eyes, "do you trust Me?"

"Why, yes, Lord," I answered, surprised.

"Then come."

He became the white Eagle. I quickly climbed onto His back, and He began to fly. I put my arms around His neck and buried my face in the fragrant feathers of His head.

He flew...and flew...and flew...until He flew into deep darkness.

# 8

# The Corrupted Strata

I COULD NOT DISCERN if it was densely dark or if it only seemed that dark because we had come from a place so permeated with light.

## The Sheepfold

THE WHITE EAGLE flew down into a walled-in area that had a shelter within it. The wall was of uncut stones and fairly high. On top of the wall were branches brandishing large, painful-looking thorns.

It was a sheepfold.[1] It was Christ's outpost in that corrupted strata occupied by Satan.[2] The enclosed area had but one gate. It appeared that the thorns were not so much to make entry by the demons impossible, but to serve as a warning. NO TRESPASSING—a visible command from Christ Himself. The sheepfold was His territory.

It occurred to me that perhaps one of the reasons the crown of thorns was crammed into Jesus' skull before His crucifixion was as a private slap in the face from Satan, for the sheepfold was crowned with thorns. Christ had dared to establish a place of safety within the enemy's hostile kingdom. That crown of thorns was an affront before His crucifixion; now, after His resurrection, it was an ever-present reminder of Christ's victory and His eternal lordship.

The white Eagle changed into the Lord.

There was scant light except for that which came from Him. "Stay with Me," He said. He had a tall staff in His hand.[3]

By the gate were two pairs of porpoise shoes that were dyed red.[4] He put on a pair, and so did I.

"Touch nothing here, Anna; all is defiled."[5] We walked out the gate into the darkness. Jesus Himself was the light on our way.

Weeping and sardonic laughter came from the darkness. They were human voices, but they sounded as if they were coming from animals.[6] Alarm gripped me. I stayed close to the Lord, walking in His footsteps. Although it was dark, I began to see dimly.

## The Outskirts of the Strata

THE SURFACE ON which we were walking was dank and sticky. There was a slight suction created on the bottoms of my shoes as we walked, as though I might become glued to the spot if I did not keep moving. Huge, slimy creatures would half roar, then lift themselves up and move threateningly toward us. They looked like giant slugs, but acted more like bull seals protecting their territory.[7] They tried to frighten us, but they ended up bowing before Jesus, a begrudging acknowledgment of His lordship.[8]

## The River of Filth

WE CAME TO a levee that sloped down to a black lagoon. The water was filthy, sluggish, and stagnant.[9] The smell was putrid.

Jesus helped me into a long pirogue. I sat down, but He stood and poled us across this narrow waterway with His staff. The water boiled and emitted steam every time His staff plunged into it.

Jesus said, "This is a river of filth. As the river of life is clear, so this one is putrid and defiling. It issues from the mouths of sinful man. As rivers of living water come from the belly of My righteous ones, so out of the blackened heart, through the mouth, comes this watery filth."

I could see creatures lying on the banks and hear them breathing. They appeared to be crocodiles, but they made blowing sounds through their nostrils like hippos.[10] Their eyes shone in the dark.

## The Chained Ones

CAVES LINED THE levees, and an occasional cry or moan came from them. I felt that the sounds I had heard when we walked through the gate came from these caves. They looked like dungeons with demons guarding the entrances. But who or what was imprisoned there?

The demons uttered low, guttural chuckles at the obvious pain of those imprisoned. They enjoyed someone else's pain.[11]

"Observe the misery," the Lord said. "My people participate in this, enjoying the downfall of another, laughing at the mistakes of others, and holding them in their chains instead of setting the captives free."[12]

I looked toward the dark entrances of the caves. Within these dungeons the enemy held captive certain areas in the lives of humans on earth. Christians, instead of helping to set the captive free, were tightening the chains of condemnation that held them in bondage. Christians were siding with the jailers against the Lord by nullifying the provision of forgiveness and reconciliation that He had made for them through His shed blood.

## The Levee

WE STEPPED ONTO the opposite bank and began to walk up a wide path to the crest of that levee. Moans came from every demon we passed. Christ's appearance among the demons tormented them, and they ran away from Him.[13]

"Light is very painful to them," Jesus said, indicating the fleeing demons. "They suck up darkness and breathe out venom—lost, corrupted forever, darkness inside and out. These who once ate the food of angels, these who stood in My Father's light, these who knew the companionship of the trustworthy—now they slither and cringe from the light, cursing the darkness and cursing the light—they are doubly damned. They eat vomit—three or four times over." (I felt that He was equating vomit with slander.) "In community with those of their kind, they laugh at each other's misery and deny each other relief—turning, forever turning upon one another, therefore always alone."

"Leave us," a voice said, and a hyena giggled.

As we topped the levee, the land as far as I could see was slimy mud, a murky wasteland.[14]

"Wet," Jesus said, "for they fear the fire. They are tormented even by dry places."

Numerous dead trees stood within the mud.

"The trees are a memorial to the vile groves of false gods. Here these trees are seen for what they actually are: broken, bare, without life—the home of snakes and birds of prey."

## Counterfeit Unity

INDEED, BLACK SNAKES were in these dead trees, as well as covering the brackish mire. They were hissing and writhing, constantly moving over one another as if mating.[15] *A false unity, a joining in the black mind,* I thought. It occurred to me that as the Lord is bringing together a oneness in Himself, so the devil is birthing a counterfeit unity.

Jesus spoke, "The spawn of demons. How Satan promotes his imitation fruit. These goad tormented souls to vomit forth slanders, lies, and cursing—rivers of putrid water in which the demons swim."

His ear caught the sound of a cry from a cave by the lagoon. He turned His head to hear, saying, "There are labyrinths also within some believers: dark corridors where the light has not shown, hutches that have not been delivered from darkness.[16] But the true light is ready to travel every corridor and touch every dark corner so that all within each believer may be of the light. Darkness is heavy with sin; it is dense and murky. My freedom is light. For the redeemed, all within them must be delivered over to light. Light must flood every corridor, and every lurking malady must be healed."

Jesus then took my hand, saying, "Come."

## The Demonic Temple

SUDDENLY WE WERE within some sort of huge temple.[17] Large, gray concrete pillars supported this main area. The room was hazy with incense, and the cloying odor of blood was mixed with that smell.

Around the perimeter were several stories of rooms, some closed and some open. They looked like caves of horn.[18] It was possible to reach only the lower rooms by foot; all the others required flight, like bats.

There were six staggered levels of rooms on the left side: six at the back and six on the right side. But how many cave rooms were there in all, I could not tell.

I could see black creatures covering the walls of the hollow rooms that were open. They looked like dark, unhealthy jellyfish, each with only one eye. These were like a fungus on the walls. Their eyes were constantly looking to and fro. Nothing escaped their notice.

# The Corrupted Strata

## Stolen Treasure

THE LORD SPOKE, "The enemy has hidden stolen treasure within the darkness of these rooms. Prying eyes guard this treasure. These spies are rewarded for their vigilance. The infested caves are a vortex, throbbing with suspicion. Here there is fear of exposure—the opposite of covering—because of love. The time has not yet come, Anna, to release these captives from the caves [meaning the stolen treasure], but all that is of Me and is Mine will be cleansed and come to Me."

I did not understand what He meant. He continued, "Just as tears and prayers can be stored above, so can praise be taken captive by the evil one and stored in caves of horn. The enemy bathes in stolen worship—renewing himself in that which belongs to God, putting his hands all over that which is sacred and secret. Since Satan cannot create but only imitate and defile that which belongs to God, his greatest joy is to desecrate that which is of the Light. My Father will one day have all that belongs to Him. The temple vessels were captured and hidden away in Babylon, desecrated by being mocked and used to toast false gods. Just as these were returned and reconsecrated to God, so all that belongs to My Father will be cleansed and consecrated to Him alone.[19] The enemy is in dense darkness, doing that which is foul in order to relieve his pain, but instead only multiplies his pain. But My Father will set free all that belongs to Him. He will cleanse it from the filth of deception and idolatry corrupting it so that it might rise to Him."

I saw demons flying into these caves of horn to defile the hidden things of God there, like spiders sucking the life out of their captured prey.

## Promised Day of Deliverance

JESUS CONTINUED, "THERE is coming a time when God Himself will raise His sword in the midheaven.[20] He will come forth in His own behalf; the fat from false sacrifices and from offerings to other gods, who are not gods, will be His.[21] The fat is His, and they have robbed Him. The praise is His, and they have stolen it from Him. They have stored it for themselves. But He will raise His sword to sever the fat from them and to release the praise stored for generations. A great holocaust will occur when the fat of many generations finally rises to Him. When He unsheathes His sword and rises up in His own behalf, none can say to Him, 'Nay!' None can call to Him, 'Hold!' None can turn Him back at the gate. He will cleanse the midheaven and set it free. Then His Light will touch every corner and purge the malignant growth from generations of corruption, thievery, and lies.[22] When He lifts His sword and releases His Light, surrogates will flee like roaches; mighty ones in the strength of wickedness will shrivel and slither away."

He spoke to the midheaven, "O promised day of deliverance, a time has been appointed, and you will be free." He turned back to me and said, "When He raises His sword in heaven, praise will be released like a bird from a cage, never to be imprisoned again."

## The Demonic Masquerade

WE BEGAN TO hear a drone, like that of bees swarming or flies gathering on a dead carcass, coming from a distant area of the temple. As those creating the monotonous sound drew nearer, I could hear the hypnotic rhythm more clearly. They were chanting a mantra.[23]

Suddenly they burst into view. It was a large and lavish procession accompanied by loud, discordant music.

The massive concrete columns within the temple obscured our presence from those entering, so we stepped out of view.

Dancers and musicians came before a woman splendidly dressed.[24] Jewels adorned her long robe and crown. She held innumerable chains in her hands just as a person would hold dog leashes. Shackles were around the necks of demonic beings she held captive, who bowed continually, kissing the ground where she walked.[25] They looked like naked humans.

Her retinue was very large and seemed to comprise those from various nations—perhaps every nation. She turned in our direction. Her eyes were red with false fire; when she opened her mouth, fire came from it.[26] We were too far away for the fire to touch us, however. When the fire ceased, honey dripped from her mouth; those in chains licked up the drops that fell to the ground.

She went up by stairs to a high throne in this incense-filled hall.[27] When she sat, her attendants wrapped the long train of her robe around her feet. The train looked like a python.[28] Those in chains groveled on either side of her throne.

## False Homage

THE KINGS OF the earth came with presents for this woman.[29] They also brought jugglers, prophets, and magicians to entertain her and her court.

The team of jugglers juggled all manner of objects of unequal weight, including gold bars and apes. But the object that fascinated me the most was a cage on which was written THE SOULS OF MEN.[30]

The prophets were almost as showy, jumping around and speaking great boasts concerning her and others present.[31] Those gathered would laugh and throw money to these false prophets.

The showiest of all, however, were the magicians, who looked extremely grave, wise, and dignified; they performed mighty signs and wonders.[32] Everyone clapped and bowed before them in awe.

Each king would take a golden coin from this woman's tongue like tokens taken while standing in line at a store counter. A number was on each coin. They would return them to her later as she went from side room to side room, servicing these kings like a prostitute with many clients.[33]

The woman's face was old and caked with makeup, but from a distance she looked beautiful and splendid. She was drinking from a jewel encrusted cup, and her eyes looked glazed.[34]

"Who is this?" I asked the Lord.

"The false church," He replied.[35] "She makes herself a queen, and those enslaved eat of the honey from her mouth. She has given herself to every demon. She services them. Many will go with her."

I looked at her, horrified.

"I have brought you to see the false masquerading as the true," He said. "Mark well the content. Mark well the consequences and outworking of the decision to embrace the darkness instead of the light. All manner of corruption breeds in darkness. Come," He said, and once again He became the white Eagle. "We go now to the bowels of the dragon."

# 9

# Bowels of the Dragon

THE WHITE EAGLE flew into a darkened tunnel that seemed to be a passageway through a mountain, but the walls were like part of a living organism, resembling an intestine. The sides of the walls seemed packed with fecal matter, and the stench was nauseating and overpowering.[1]

## An Attack: The Flesh

ALTHOUGH I WAS with the white Eagle, the filth and blackness shocked me. I was afraid. I tried to maintain some sort of spiritual equilibrium, but fear began to paralyze my faith.

Hopelessness, oppression, and despair were within the very walls of this tunnel. I knew that Jesus was protecting me, but the presence of evil was suffocating.

Then, like a trapped animal, my mind began to search for an escape: *Where am I going? Why am I here? What if I fall off in this place? How can I get out of here?*

Once doubt had gained an entrance, panic soon followed, by-passing all assurance of the Lord's protection. Now, thoughts like wild dogs began to lunge at me. Did they come from within or from the tunnel? I did not know, but I was frantic with fear: *I won't make it; I can't hold on. They'll hurt me. They'll kill me!*[2]

If the Lord had not shielded me, I believe these thoughts would have torn me to shreds. I clung to the white Eagle. "Jesus, Son of David," I cried, "have mercy upon me."[3]

I could not tell what happened, but slowly the sense of almost being eaten alive lessened. Jesus, my Savior, had come forth in me. He had shown mercy.

I was in shock, though, and dazed, rather like a person who has been attacked by a pack of ravenous wolves and escaped only with her life. I was left weakened and trembling, badly shaken.

The Lord strengthened me, and I sighed, relaxing my grip somewhat.[4] He would protect me. He would not let me fall.

"I am all right," I sighed. "I am all right." My trust in God had returned.

Then silently, more like vapors than thoughts, insinuations reached for me like tendrils of smoke.

## An Attack: The World

IT HAS ALWAYS seemed strange to me that after a severe attack by the enemy, the most dangerous period of time appears to be after the battle is over and the victory secured. Perhaps one is vulnerable because of weariness, allowing vigilance against attack to be relaxed. But stranger than this is the fact that after the heat of battle, I always forget this truth.

I forgot again.

The insinuations reaching for me were disarmingly subtle; they made the world, which is Satan's heaven, seem to be all that I could ever desire or should ever desire.[5] Promises sweeter than honey enveloped me, promises of having Satan's heaven now and God's heaven later.

Suddenly the tunnel lost its stench; instead, it emitted a tantalizing fragrance. I thought to myself, *Why am I doing this? I can have anything I want simply by applying myself. I don't need to live like this. In fact, I'm tired of living like this.*

I began to think of ways to make money—and not just to make money, but to make a fortune. *Only a fortune can lift me above this sort of trial,* I thought. *Only a fortune can give me luxuries commensurate with my taste, which deserves to be expressed and enjoyed. There is so much beauty in the world, and I want to surround myself with this loveliness. There's nothing wrong in that. I can do it with hard work. All I need to do is to center myself upon this goal and head for it, give myself to it...head for it and give myself to it...head for it and give myself to it...*

"Wait, wait," I said to myself. "This isn't right. Giving myself to a life of accumulation, just satisfying my senses, can't be right." Such an idea was a siren song whose allure, if it did not bring shipwreck, certainly would have seduced me into a spiritual limp. Deadly.

"No!" I said silently. "Choose you this day whom you will serve, and I choose Christ. I choose Christ," I cried aloud.[6]

The vaporous fingers ceased reaching for me and silently slid away. Again, the Lord strengthened me. I sighed deeply as before, relieved.

## An Attack: The Devil

BY THIS TIME I thought I saw some light at the end of the tunnel. I started to become anxious for relief. I wanted out. Out.

Then, as if in my own voice, I heard, "Jesus may love you, but it's a strange sort of love that would bring you into a place of such great danger. And I can't see that He's protecting you as He should. Of course, if He'd told you beforehand what you would be facing... but He didn't. If you could acquire more knowledge yourself, you wouldn't need to rely upon Him for protection. You could protect yourself. You deserve better than this."

There it was: pride, presumption, unbelief, accusations against the Lord's lovingkindness, and an invitation to be independent of Him, better than Him—in other words, rebellion. All of these were the deep things of Satan.[7]

"Oh, God," I said within myself, "forgive me. That I would think I could do anything by myself, when I know that apart from You there is no life. I love You, and I know that You love me. You alone are the victor, You alone. You alone will do all and be all and are all; I trust You, my Savior and my Lord, my God in whom I trust."[8]

With great passion I cried out within the tunnel: "I have been crucified with Christ, and it is no longer I who live, but Christ lives in me!"[9]

## The Gigantic Cavern

JOYOUSLY THE WHITE Eagle burst through the far mouth of the tunnel. Now we seemed to be flying inside a gigantic cavern within that mountain, but I could not be sure, for I was unable to see the top. Within this cavern, if it was a cavern, the atmosphere was gray and deathly still, but electric, as it might be in the eye of a hurricane.

Tunnels honeycombed the encircling mountain, both up high, as was the one we had traveled, and at the base.

## Satan's Palace

JUST AHEAD OF us was another mountain rising from within the center of this cavern. It looked as though it was made of shiny, jagged coal. On its top was an exquisite palace, as perfect and lustrous as a jet gemstone. A thick, yellow liquid oozed from beneath the structure and slid down the mountain. The air reaked of sulfur.[10]

At the base of this mountain, large red dragons luxuriated in a cesspool moat, as wild beasts might cool themselves in muddy water on the Serengeti.[11] Their heads rested against the base of the mountain. Slight fire would come from their nostrils; when this fire touched the yellow liquid sliding down the mountain, a flame would ignite but quickly go out. They rolled their eyes up at us, but we must have been outside of their designated patrol area, for we did not raise their ire enough to protect the castle.

The palace itself was ingenious in design—imaginative and tasteful, but dark, cold, uninviting, and foreboding.

"Satan's mountain and his palace," the white Eagle said.[12–13] He continued to fly toward it.

## Attack of the Harpies

SUDDENLY, DARK ANGELS by the thousands poured out from the tunnels and began encircling us, like bats leaving caves at sunset. They had the heads and torsos of women and the wings, tails, legs, and clawed feet of rapacious vultures.[14]

"They cannot touch us," the white Eagle said. "Remain calm."

These harpies would pass by us closely, crying and taunting, but they never obstructed our view of the palace nor hindered the white Eagle's relentless flight toward it.

## The Prince of Darkness

HIGH IN THE black palace at a lightless window, a solitary figure appeared, looking at us.[15] From a distance, one could sense his power, authority, and extreme loneliness. Yes—loneliness—separation, isolation, and a cold, cold heart.

He looked like a Spanish prince. He wore an elegant black velvet robe encrusted with jewels; he was tastefully and perfectly groomed. He was handsome, almost perfectly handsome, with shiny black hair and dark intelligent eyes.

He waved his hand, and the harpies flew away as quickly as they had come, retreating into the honeycomb of tunnels. The sound of thousands of leathery wings dwindled away, leaving the cavern quiet in comparison.

After that he continued to stand unmoving at the window, his eyes fixed upon us: lonely, like a king who is also a rejected lover.

I thought to myself, *There he is: he who was so full of light that he was named 'the shining one'—now 'the prince of darkness,' he whose executive ability still is such that he manages a vast, global empire of deceit, seducing the whole world.*

Seeing his impeccable, ageless beauty, I could not help wondering what he must have been like before his fall, for he was created sublime in order to hold the most exalted position in the heavenly court. He was "the anointed cherub who covers."[16] I wondered if once there were three cherubs guarding the throne of God, one on either side and one above? Was that why he was created so beautiful, wise, and powerful? To guard the throne from that elevated position?

He walked amid the coals of fire, sharing the very heart of God, intimate with the Godhead. Did he betray the One who loved him by striking at Him from above? Is that the reason he boasted that he would exalt his throne above the stars of God?[17]

*There he is,* I thought to myself, *still superior, but superior now only in evil, and because of his vaulting pride, isolated— beyond mercy's reach and beyond asking for it.*

The white Eagle turned from the palace and began to fly back toward the tunnel.

## Taunts of the Black Raven

A HUGE BLACK raven suddenly appeared beside us.[18] Its feathers were a brilliant ebony, and its eyes flashed a fiery red. "Why have You come?" hissed Satan. "Does it please You to shame me before my subjects? Does it please You to bring love and warmth here to torment us? You are cruel!"

The Lord said nothing.

"Don't You miss me?" Satan continued. "Did You come here because of Your loneliness for me? Would You like to come here more often to be with me, just to see me?" The raven cracked a hard, cruel laugh. "You miss me and love me still," he exulted. Then in tones venomous with bitter scorn, he mocked: "You are a fool to love me even now, Jesus of Nazareth."[19]

The Lord's silence infuriated the raven.

"Don't come back to shame me before my subjects! I am king here. Stay away! I don't love You, and I wish all manner of exquisite torments upon You to express my contempt. Stay away!" Satan spewed vehemently.[20]

Having said that, the raven made a sharp turn and flew back to the palace.

The white Eagle continued through the tunnel from which we had come. A void, deathly silence was in that darkness now.

## Return to the Sheepfold

HE FLEW TO the sheepfold and stopped before the gate. I climbed down from His back. He became the Lord again with His shepherd's staff in His hand. He opened the gate and led me inside.

We both removed our shoes and stood barefoot within the sheepfold. I was shivering, and He put His arm around me.

"It is all right, Anna," He said. "You needed to see that Satan is cruel. Rest now."

Warmth began to flow into me, and I tried to breathe deeply, settling myself.

"Why did You show me these things?" I asked.

"To you it has been granted to know," He said. "Mark well what you have seen and heard."

## The Vision of Judgment

"LOOK," HE CONTINUED, gesturing toward the ground in front

of us within the sheepfold. The area opened to reveal the world spinning some distance beneath us.

As I looked at the globe, I heard huge footsteps, as if giants were walking, shaking the earth.[21] The ground of earth trembled, and mountains began to break apart.

"Look again," He said, gesturing above Him.

Heaven opened, and I saw something dropping from the center of the bright angels.

"What is it?" I asked.

"A plumbline," He answered.[22] The weighted plumbline dropped from heaven through the sheepfold to the earth.

"Our great God has relented twice before, but now He has dropped the plumbline."[23]

As the plumbline reached earth, great rejoicing began in heaven. It was as though every created being there was singing, and the sound began to shake the celestial realms:

> His righteousness is from everlasting to everlasting.
> His judgments are sure and will be withheld no longer.

As the thunderous rejoicing increased, fire came out of heaven and traveled the plumbline, passing before us and sweeping down the line to the earth. Suddenly the whole world was aflame.[24]

## The False Church Judged

AS THE CHANT in heaven continued, Jesus spoke, "Edom will be judged.[25] To the world she looked pure, but she will be stubble before the wrath of God. The children of the living God will see Him on His holy mount. But to the church of Edom, He will hide Himself in darkness, never to reveal Himself again.

"The mountain of Edom will melt like wax before the flame of the Lord, but the righteous will thrive amid the flames. Indeed, the righteous will be a flame before the Lord.

"The righteous will be counted as nothing by the enemies

of our God. They will be mocked, a crown of thorns pressed into their brows, but God, our God, will consume the thorns with His fire and heal their wounds with His balm.

"The plumbline has dropped. The earth shakes as giants walk the land. God's power will be seen. No giant can stand before His power. No giant can walk into His flame. The righteous will look up and rejoice with the whole assembly of heaven. In one mighty chorus they will proclaim His righteousness and His power. His justice will prevail, for the plumbline has dropped and will not be removed.

"Fear, O you who lie with the adder, you who drink the venom of vipers. The day is coming and now is when the Word of the Lord will cut you in two, and you will writhe in the agony consigned to those who embrace idols.

"The heavens proclaim His righteousness and His throne; like a great rock, He will fall upon the wicked. The righteous will look upon His face, but deep darkness will shroud Him from the eyes of Esau.[26]

"Woe to those who embrace idols. They couple themselves with demons. Fire has traveled the plumbline. Lightning has flashed from His hand. Indeed, the world will see it but will remain deceived. When giants walk the land, the mountains tremble; but when God walks the land, the mountains melt.

"As the chant of God's righteousness goes forth in heaven, there is a splitting, a separation, a falling away, and a letting go: ruin follows the reverberation of that refrain. Division that could not be measured until the plumbline dropped from heaven to earth.[27] All of heaven has joined in the song, and all of earth will hear and not hear. Judgments are in the land. The righteous will grow in righteousness, and the wicked will gnash their teeth and curse God.

"Hold fast to God, Anna. Hold fast to God. Once He relented, even twice, but now judgments have begun with the household of God.[28] The righteous will shine like the sun, and the corrupt church, rich though she be, bedecked in beautiful gifts from God, will be stubble before Him.[29] For He will relent no longer, and the mountain of Esau will be leveled. A man will kick at the dust of that mountain and say 'Where is she? Not even a mound as high as an ant hill remains. Where is she?' Her rocks and earth will have been ground to powder and blown away. In her place there will be a desert wasteland that none will turn aside to see because nothing will remain.

"The mountain of the Lord: the righteous will see it and be glad.[30] They will join in the mighty chorus of heaven. They will walk the streets of gold and feed upon the manna.[31] They will stand beside the plumbline and not be ashamed. Righteousness and justice are the foundation of Your throne, O righteous God.

"O Just and True, mankind has thought itself more just than You; but to the righteous You will reveal Your righteousness, and to the just, You will reveal how just You have always been."[32]

## Join the Chorus

THE LORD CONTINUED, "Join the chorus of the sons of God. Proclaim His righteousness forevermore. Let the sound of our cry fill the sky. Let the sound of our cry fill the earth. Join the rejoicing as the chant goes forth, falling with a weight mightier than giant's steps, falling with the weight of the throne of God Himself.[33]

"Rejoice, O heavens; weep, O world. Rejoice, O righteous, and tremble, O flesh. For fire has come from heaven, traveling the plumbline, and only the Son of God will pass through this flame.[34] Rejoice, O heavens, and be glad, for judgments have begun; the final redemption is near. Our God will settle all accounts. The plumbline will not be removed until all lines up with the Son of God.[35] Rejoice!"

The Lord turned to me and said, "Mark well what you have seen and heard, for these things are and will be; no hand will stop them. Come."

He took my hand, and together we followed the flaming plumbline into heaven.

# 10

# The Throne of God

A S WE ROSE, the light became multicolored, vibrant, alive almost. The sound of the chant intensified a hundred-fold as we followed the flaming plumbline into the third heaven:[1]

> His righteousness is from everlasting to everlasting.
> His judgments are sure and will be withheld no longer.

### Jubilant Celebration

WHEN JESUS APPEARED on the "sea of glass," a great shout went up; those singing burst into spontaneous rejoicing at the sight of Him.[2] We had entered the third heaven at what seemed to be the back of the throne room.

The redeemed began to dance as one—sidestepping in a swift, gliding movement, as dancers on earth might in an old-fashioned courante.[3] The movements were vigorous and joyful. Those passing near us would reach out a hand to touch Jesus; He reached out to touch hand after hand of those passing by in the dance. All were laughing. I was certain the dance was spontaneous. The redeemed were dancing by the power of the Holy Spirit, thousands upon thousands led by the Spirit Himself.[4]

Jesus glanced over at me. "I am needed, Anna," He said. He motioned for someone to draw nearer to us. It was the large formal angel whom I had met on the moving path. As the Lord spoke to me, He was still smiling and touching the hands extended to Him. "Epaggelias will be with you."[5]

## The Angel Epaggelias

SO THAT IS *his name*, I thought to myself, smiling inwardly.

The angel bowed from the waist to Jesus. The Lord smiled at me, reached over and squeezed my hand, and was gone.

Epaggelias and I continued to watch the exuberant dancing.

"You have come at a joyous time," Epaggelias said.

"Why?" I asked.

He answered, "We rejoice daily for those who have recently come into the kingdom, but this celebration is in response to your Father's proclamation that a great ingathering is about to commence.[6-7] His children are filled with thanksgiving to Him for His faithfulness, for He is about to do a quick work and redeem many of their brothers and sisters through Christ Jesus our Lord."

"That is exciting," I smiled. "Thank you for telling me, Epaggelias."

He bowed in acknowledgment and smiled in spite of himself, for it was a private joke between the two of us that Jesus had just given me his name.

# The Throne of God

The thousands of dancers gathered into circles, each circle containing about twenty-four dancers. They began circling and weaving in and out within the rings. Some were laughing, but everywhere there was rejoicing. They began to sing as they danced:

> Again and again we sing of His glory,
> Again and again rejoice in our God.

All were executing the same movements, twirling and whirling within the circles, and singing the same song everywhere on the sea of glass.

## Silent Worship

THEN, AS BY the Spirit's leading, the music slowed to a sigh, a pause, a selah.[8] The redeemed paused also, silently with arms raised, abandoned to God. I remembered Psalm 65 where it states, "There will be silence before You...praise in Zion, O God." Silent worship.

After a long pause, a slow, stately melody began. Besides the tone of the instruments I recognized, some of the music was being played on instruments I had never heard.[9] Perhaps they were from other cultures or of ancient design. In harmony with the instrumental music was another lovely sound. It was not singing, nor was it being played by musicians. What was it?

## Dance of Worship

THE REDEEMED RESPONDED to the music by beginning a majestic dance of worship. The movements were regal and noble, and they executed them with great care and intensity. Perhaps a pavane is the dance on earth most closely resembling this worship of the redeemed.[10] I felt they were dancing to express their respect. Their dancing was homage. The change of pace allowed me to get my bearings.

## The Throne of God

THE THRONE ROOM was as brilliant with light as Satan's kingdom had been dark.

The surface on which the redeemed were dancing was a pavement of light that looked like a translucent blue. The area was as immense as a huge plaza. At the far end of this expansive "sea" was a dazzling white light, in the center of which was the throne of God.[11]

A great yearning welled up within me, and a whisper involuntarily escaped: "Daddy." His presence drew me with the cords of love. Epaggelias looked down at me and smiled.

The Father's being is manifested by light of an indescribable whiteness. His uncreated glory radiates outward in all directions to form a great sphere of awesome colors.[12] From a considerable distance this radiance looks like an eye with a dazzling white pupil. Perhaps the sphere is due to the reflection upon the sea of glass. I could not tell. But I remembered that often the early church had mosaics or frescoes of the "eye of God" in its buildings.[13] Standing on the sea of glass, I wondered if they were seeking to depict the glory of the Father as well as His omniscience.

The splendor of His person radiates out into bands of color, like a bow whose hues blend from white to yellow, to gold, to the Shekinah reddish-gold, and on through the color spectrum of reds, purples, blues, and ending with green.[14] The rainbow on earth is a type of "My [God's] bow."[15]

## Moving Closer to the Throne

TRANSFIXED, I WAS lost in the wonder of Him. Epaggelias touched my shoulder to draw my attention to that which he was about to say. "Come with me," he said, and with that he began to move toward the throne area. We began to pass through those worshiping, sometimes ducking beneath a dancer's arm as we made our way forward.

The light into which we were entering began to intensify, as well as the sense of power. As we moved nearer to the throne, the radiance looked more like the waves of light in the aurora borealis when it forms an arc of lights across the sky.[16]

The blazing light was not blinding as would be the earth's sun if you gazed at it. One could experience, feel, and even look at this light.[17]

## Angelic Praise

THOUSANDS OF ANGELS were circling above the throne area, and thousands more seemed to be arriving to join them.

Countless numbers of angels were already within the bow of the corona around the throne. Each group wore the color of that particular hue. They were making musical sounds by flying at different levels and speeds and patterns.[18] Just as a whirling stick might make a different sound—increasingly higher or louder by the speed with which it is whirled—so these angels in their flying brought forth various sounds of praise. The tones that their flight made were different from singing or the playing of instruments. This must have been the musical sound whose origin I could not detect earlier, rare in its beauty.

They seemed to be unbelievably happy, swimming, as it were, in the glory of God. I too felt this joy; forever would not be long enough to praise Him and to receive His joy back from Him.[19]

At times some angels would fly together, producing a tone different from the sound of those in flight in a single color.

## One With Praise

THE MELODIES, LIKE the light in the throne room, went right through me. The music of praise entered me and passed through me, and I became one with the sound. It was as though I became praise. I remembered that in the Book of Psalms David said, "But, I prayer"[20]—meaning that he was prayer. So it is with praise in the throne room.

Epaggelias paused amid the dancers and spoke, "The harmony, the unity, and the desire of these here to give to the Father His due—constantly giving of themselves and receiving more of Him when they praise and adore—bring forth a sweet music."

"Yes," I agreed.

We watched and listened a moment before moving forward again.

As we drew nearer to the throne, it was as though I began to see praise.[21] It was translucent, almost invisible, but I could see it. It seemed to have different properties. Some kinds of praise were like fabric, some like particles. Thanksgivings looked similar to bird flights of light.

## Praise Purified

THE ANGELS IN flight gathered some of the praise from the sea of glass and wove it into their praise within each color of the bow (that is, the radiance around the Father) before it went to Him. Some worship went to a small altar on which there appeared to be smoldering coals.[22] I wondered why some went one way and some another.

Epaggelias addressed this unspoken question. "Some praise is already in harmony with heavenly praise, but some must pass through the fire," he said.[23]

## Angels of His Presence

ANGELIC BEINGS IN pale lavender were at this small altar. Their robes were embroidered with deep purple and gold on the sleeves and hem, and they were bound with golden girdles. The palms of their hands were also tinted with the purple color. I felt that they must be angels of His presence.[24] They took great care with all that was going to the Father. There was a delicacy in handling that which belongs to Him, like a shepherd encouraging and assisting a newborn lamb. Whether being woven into the angelic harmony within each color of the radiance, or like a homing pigeon, drawn into the coals on the small altar—all, all goes to Him.[25] Nothing is carried away nor stolen.

## Interwovenness

I BECAME MORE aware of the pleasant fragrance around the throne area and of the interwovenness of sound and color and smell.[26-27] These cannot be woven together on earth the way they are blended here in heaven. We below can experience them simultaneously, but above they seem to have the same properties. It is more like water being poured into water. Water, having the same properties, can be mixed. So it is here with sound, light, and fragrance. It seems strange to see sound, hear color, and for smell to have a tangible quality to it; yet in heaven it all seems natural and right and even obvious.

## Seven Great Flames

THERE WERE SEVEN great flames of fire, seven torches, before the throne.[28]

Epaggelias spoke, "These are manifestations of the Holy Spirit. They burn before the throne continually. He reveals Himself here [above] and on earth. The Lamb embodies these, and the Spirit takes of Him. Of the created, heavenly hosts, the seraphim, burning in holiness, most closely resemble these lamps of the Spirit.[29] They burn above, and the lamps burn before [the throne]."

## Seraphim

I LOOKED UP to see heavenly beings burning right above the most intense light of the throne. Each had six wings. Now and then I could see their faces or the movement of their wings. They burned like blow torches. From them came the sweetest and purest music I had ever heard.

## The Twenty-four Elders

IN THE MIDST of the intensely white light of the throne area, there stood twenty-four very tall beings with crowns on their heads.[30] Each wore a chain with a single gold medallion hanging from it. The hair on their heads was white, and they were full of light. I could sense that they were ancient, wise, and bore much authority.

Epaggelias led me into a clear area nearer the throne.

## Four Living Creatures

WITHIN THE GREATER light, I could see four living creatures.[31] Each was whiter than white, so full of light were they. Each had six wings. One looked like a calf, one like a lion, one like an eagle, and one like a man. Their heads and their feet, paws, hoofs, or claws were golden. They were full of eyes, awesome and very beautiful.

The living creature of light that looked something like a man wore a transparent garment with a collar that came up high from the neck to the ears. This collar looked like an open fan of white lace interwoven with golden thread. A golden yoke and front panel completed the center of the robe. Through the gossamer fabric of his clothing, I could see that his body was covered with eyes. Beneath the wings of each of these living creatures were hands.

When the redeemed dropped to their knees during the dance, these four bowed before the King.[32] Within their hands they held golden bowls that they presented before the throne.[33]

Epaggelias spoke to me: "These represent four great divisions of animate creation.[34] The Word says that all things are to praise Him.[35] These are the remnant of creation that fulfill that Word. That which they do is attributed to all that God has made."

"Why do they have golden heads?" I whispered.

"Gold shows their place among those representing creation before the throne," he answered. "It is a precious metal on earth and representative of Christ here, so their color reflects that which is precious: worshiping God. God deals with the remnant. These four are a certain remnant. Before the throne, God the Almighty, the glorious One, is being praised and worshiped by His creation. The white represents the innocence of all He brought forth originally. It reminds Him that what He created was created pure and uncorrupted in the beginning."

## Concluding the Offering of Praise

THE OFFERING OF worship and thanksgiving by the redeemed was drawing to a close. As one, the redeemed saints stepped forward, their arms around each others' waists. They knelt on their right knees before the throne, bowing their heads in reverence. The twenty-four ancient ones and the four living creatures knelt, saying *amen* at the conclusion of the dance.[36]

The myriads of angels praising Him aloft within the radiance stood still. They looked like thousands upon thousands and tier upon tier of organ pipes as far as I could see.

In the silence that followed, God spoke.

## 11

# The Father's Lap

B EAUTIFUL, CHILDREN," GOD the Father said. "Now rest."
Those who had been dancing broke formation and
began talking among themselves in small groups. The warmth
of their fellowship was as children around an open fire in the
presence of a loving father.

Epaggelias leaned over and spoke to me. "Now watch," he said.

### The Children's Offering

AN ANGEL BEGAN to play a simple melody on a recorder as
hundreds of children came before the throne.[1] Angels and the

redeemed carried the very young in their arms. They led other children by their hands.

The children took small bouquets of flowers to Jesus and to the Father.[2] Jesus kissed each child, and both He and the Father talked with them. Huge hands of light came out from the throne area as the Father received the flowers.[3] He touched every child and blessed each one. "Thank you," the Father said to each child, calling each one of them by name.[4]

Epaggelias continued to me privately, "These are ones who died young."

Instantly I knew that some of the children had died through miscarriage, and some had been aborted; how I knew this, I do not know.

Epaggelias continued, "They are raised to maturity here. Both angels and their own brethren—the redeemed—are their tutors."

I looked from the children to search Epaggelias' face. He saw my perplexity.

"Anna, many of the mysteries of our God are unfolding now.[5] For some the book of understanding is open." He looked back at the children. "Our God can speak to the spirit of a child from conception. Its spirit can respond from the beginning of life in the womb."[6]

I too looked back at the children. I suddenly realized that John the Baptist had responded to the Spirit of the Lord from the womb.[7] If the Holy Spirit can search the mind of God Himself, as the Word says, of course the Spirit can communicate with a child's spirit even before birth.[8]

The children who had been aborted presented small branches of henna as a way of showing the Father that they had forgiven those responsible for their deaths and also asking Him to forgive them as well.[9]

As I watched, the magnitude of the fairness of our God overwhelmed me. He had given each child the opportunity to come to Christ, and all who had chosen Him were here.[10]

Epaggelias spoke, "None are lost from the hand of Jesus, Anna. None."

## Song of the Seraphim

AS THE CHILDREN began to leave, the seraphim sang:

> O Jewel beyond every jewel, our God,
> Prize beyond every prize.
> God eternal, God sublime,
> God before our eyes.

While looking at the intense light of the Father, my eyes had become more accustomed to the brilliance, I suppose, for as the children began to clear the throne area, I could see more of the throne itself.

## The Throne

BENEATH THE ARMREST of the throne on either side were two very large cherubim.[11] They were looking out at me through the blazing light. Each cherub seemed to be a composite of the four creatures represented in the living creatures. Each had the face of a man, the wings of an eagle, and one portion of each body was that of a lion and the other part that of an ox. They guarded either side of the throne of God. They were exquisite and so impregnated with light that they were like lightning with a pale lavender light defining their shape.

The throne on which the Father was sitting was bejeweled with intangibles: righteousness, justice, holiness, mercy, and other virtues.[12]

## The Priceless Above

EPAGGELIAS SPOKE AS he saw me gazing more intently into the light surrounding the throne, "It is the things that are not that are in heaven, Anna."

I felt that he meant the things that are not tangible.

Epaggelias continued, "The priceless is uncreated. These the enemy wants, for their value is beyond gold. He will give mere gold and silver for them, but it is not a fair exchange. Wisdom, prudence, joy, peace, truthfulness, faithfulness— these adorn the throne of the almighty One. Mere jewels cannot compare. The streets here are gold, but faith is a jewel beyond compare, mercy a commodity more precious than diamonds."[13]

I looked into the awesome light of our God. "Daddy," I whispered again.

## The Father

WITHIN THE RESPLENDENT light, part of my Father's form could be seen.[14] I could see what appeared to be His feet and that which looked like a garment falling in drapes to the sea of glass. Flashes of lightning were in this garment.[15] Within the searing light, I could see something of His hands and the loose sleeves covering His arms. Above His waist, the light emanating from Him was so blinding in its intensity, purity, and holiness that I could see no further.[16]

As Jesus was handing the last baby back to an angel who would carry it from the throne room, my Father spoke to me.

"Anna, My child," He said.

Jesus turned to smile at me. Epaggelias gestured for me to move forward, closer to the throne.

## Standing Before the Father

I DID SO, rubber-legged, moving nearer to that all-consuming light. After I got to the area where the children had been, I dropped to my knees and bowed my face to the sea of glass.[17]

Jesus stepped over to me and helped me to rise, strengthening me as He did so. "My sister is here to see You, Father."

As I rose to my feet, the Father's arms of light came out from all that splendor and picked me up, lifting me high into the air. The action seemed as natural as a father picking up his child.

## Our Father's Lap

HE SET ME on His lap.[18]

I was so overwhelmed with love and gratitude and relief, that without thinking, I held up my arms and buried my face into the light. The response was like that of a child who would bury its face in the parent's clothing.

"Daddy," I said, sensing peace, unbelievable peace.

"You are precious to Me, Anna."

"I love You, Daddy."

"And I love you, Anna," He said, drawing me closer.

As we sat there enjoying one another, He began to address my innermost thoughts.

## Hope

HE SAID, "THOSE who are called to draw near to Me will share in My peace.[19] But only those who have hope have peace, continual peace.[20] If hope is gone, the soul is tossed to and fro seeking safe harbor, Anna. I want My children's eyes set on Me, hoping in Me, not looking at the passing panorama of earthly events being played out before them. I want them to look beyond, to look up, to see at last the distant shore toward which they are sailing, filling their hearts and minds, their eyes and ears with Me. This will bring the hope that gives peace."

I sat up and looked into the greater light of the area that would be His face if I could have seen it.

## Deeper Into God

MY FATHER CONTINUED, "If they delight in Me, Anna, their desires will carry them deeper into Me. Then, as they are drawn into Me, so will they leave the earth's orbit in greater and greater degrees. Soon, like gravity, the pull from My realm, the desire for Me—to know Me and to experience the eternal while in the temporal—will become so strong that they will be set free from earth's orbit and will be drawn more and more swiftly into Mine.[21] I do not wish to dwell in a dark cloud any longer.[22] I want My children to know their Father. I want them to see Me and hear Me, for I am a loving Father to them, Anna, and I care for every breath they take. Truth, who is My Son, came into the world. Many have 'seen' and walked out of the prison doors. But My Son came to reveal Me.[23] Now that revelation will become present reality. The unfolding, the accomplishment of that earthly mission, which began with the unveiling of My Son, will reach a present clarity unaccomplished before."

## Vision of Troubled Waters

I SAW A hand moving back and forth in a pool of water, disturbing any clear reflection from being seen.

"As the waters of mankind become more and more troubled," my Father said, "the spiritual pool will become clearer."[24–25] (Then I saw a hand held over a clear pool and reflected perfectly within the water.) "My children will know Me. Will you help Me, Anna?"[26]

## Offered a Responsibility

"IF YOU NEED me, Daddy," I said.

"I have raised you up in this hour to see into the heavenly realm, to fly in the rarified air with the white Eagle, to rest in the Eagle's nest, and to taste of the delights that are to come by eating from My hand so that you may eat and others digest what you have eaten."[27]

"How, Daddy?"

"By giving them hope by allowing them to see and experience through your eyes and experiences. I will say through you, 'Hope,' for I am doing a new thing in these days; all who hunger and thirst for Me will eat and drink. You will be My chancellor."[28]

"Like of the exchequer?" I blurted out before I knew it (for I had only heard the term mentioned in these days on the British Broadcasting Corporation).

"No," my Father laughed, "My secretary."

"Oh," I said relieved, for I thought I might be able to handle a secretarial assignment—*with the Lord's help,* I quickly added to myself.

### Letters From Home

MY FATHER CONTINUED, "You will tell of what you have seen and heard. You will reveal My heart and give hope by revealing 'home' to others.[29] Your words will be like letters from home to those in the field. When a soldier is on the battlefield, a letter from home telling of the people and places of home gives the soldier great hope. He keeps going because he longs for home and realizes that he is greatly loved. Hope, Anna, is a gift to mankind. Without hope, they languish."

"Why have You chosen me, Daddy?"

"Because you are simple, Anna, and know little. Before the foundations of the world, I called you, not because you are wise or intelligent, but because I delight in you.[30-32] My Son delights in you. The Holy Spirit delights in you. And I have brought you to Myself this day to ask for your help."

### "Yes"

"OF COURSE I will help You," I said, "but Daddy, please help me to refrain from sinning against You. I want to represent You truly. Please keep me pure so that I might not defile this gift or the trust that You have placed in me."

### Only in Him

I CONTINUED LISTENING to my Father speak to me. "In Him, Anna, in My Son. I trust only in Him.[33] It is His life, His ministry, and the work of the Holy Spirit through you. My dear child, you are completely untrustworthy.[34] As the life of My Son increases within you, it appears that you are more trustworthy, but actually, it is only Him; it always will remain only Him."[35]

The Father's Lap

He paused briefly before continuing. "Now, Anna, you must give yourself time to be with Me. Chancellors must grow into their duties and anointing and authority.[36] My child, My heart is turned toward the children. Show them My heart that they may turn toward Me."[37]

He picked me up from His lap and placed me before Him on the sea of glass as He said, "Now, stand before Me."

## The Awesome Convocation

WITHIN THE THRONE room something tremendous seemed to be happening. From all directions there was a great gathering of angels converging upon the throne area. Some that were flying had wings; some did not. There seemed to be myriads and myriads of angels aloft within the throne room, and those within the radiance joined them.

A ripple of sound began near the throne and moved out through the angelic ranks. As the tone increased, singing began until it reached a crescendo at the outer edges of the heavenly host who was in flight. It was as though whatever originated near the throne passed through the others, allowing the singing to swell and then be released outward. The sound was exhilarating:

> Praise You beyond the highest heaven.
> Praise You beyond the lowest depth.
> Praise You for Your loving presence.
> Praise You for Your judgments blest.
> Praise You, sun and moon together.
> Praise You, whirling wheels and stars.[38]
> Praise You, angel chorus sounding.
> Praise You near and praise afar.
>
> Children sing Your praises, Father.
> Maidens praise You, holy Son.
> Holy Spirit, we adore You.
> Finish now what You have begun.

> Started long ago, hallelujah,
> When together we did sing,[39]
> Blessed Father, Son, and Spirit,
> To You, O God, our praise we bring.

(The redeemed joined in the chorus.)

> Praise Your holy name, hallelujah,
> Praise Your holy name, hallelujah,
> Praise Your holy name, hallelujah,
> Praise Your holy name.

Suddenly, angels without number began blowing trumpets.[40] The sound was awesome, electrifying, glorious. As the trumpets sounded, everyone present began to proclaim fervently:

> Glory to God.
> Glory to God.
> Glory to God.
> Glory to God.

I had never been a part of anything so powerful. It took my breath away. At the end of the proclamation, the elders threw down their crowns and fell on their faces before the throne, and so did the four living creatures and all the redeemed and angels who were on the sea of glass within the throne room. I too fell on my face before God, for who could stand? The angels aloft held their places at attention.

Then one lone shofar blew.[41] It seemed that the sound echoed throughout heaven. As the sound died away, fire and peels of thunder and lightning began to belch from the throne.

God Almighty spoke, "Stand to your feet, Anna."

I stood, but I was trembling. Everyone else stood also.

# 12

# The Installation

THE THUNDER AND lightning increased within the throne, and fire streaked upward at times.[1]

## The Witness of Two

JESUS SPOKE: "FATHER, she is Mine and belongs to My kingdom.[2] She is ready to fulfill the commission You have given to her." He stepped toward me. "I verify this commissioning, for this is the witness of two. Both My Father and I witness to this."[3]

## The Golden Chain

MY FATHER'S HUGE hands of light came from the throne area and placed upon me a large golden chain made of twenty-four linked medallions.[4] An even larger center medallion hung over my heart.[5] As I looked down at the chain, I realized that beneath the chain I was wearing the multicolored robe given to me by Jesus earlier.[6]

## My Father's Name

THEN MY FATHER touched my forehead with His hand.[7] It burned like a brand. "My name is on her forehead," He said in a voice that sounded like mighty, rushing waters.[8] He reached out again with a scepter and touched my shoulders.[9] "She is My chancellor."

Jesus acknowledged, "I bear witness to this."

The Spirit, who is invisible, spoke from the left side of my Father, "I bear witness to this."[10]

## Impartation by the Ancient Ones

THEN ANOTHER VOICE spoke. "Do you trust God?"

"I do," I answered, turning to look at one of the twenty-four ancient ones around the throne.

"Come here," he said. He put his hand upon one of the golden medallions on the chain and spoke with great authority and solemnity: "All the gifts and graces given to me, I now impart to you."[11] Then he motioned for me to pass to the next ancient one, and I did.

Each one of the ancients asked me the same question as the first. Each placed his hand on a different medallion of the chain with the same impartation.

## "Your Heart Belongs to Me"

THEN MY HEAVENLY Father spoke again. "Come here," He said.

## The Installation

"Look at the insignias." The gold of the twenty-four medallions was shining like diamonds under an intense light. "The gifts and graces that are Christ are yours," He said.[12] Then He put His hand upon the center medallion and said with great tenderness, "Your heart belongs to Me. Your heart belongs to Me. Your heart belongs to Me."[13]

## The Finger of God

AFTER THIS HE touched my eyes with His forefingers. It was like lightning shooting through me. "The finger of God has touched your eyes, Anna."[14] Then He put the lower part of the palms of His hands upon my eyes, and the power almost bent me over backward.[15] He moved His hands and placed His fingers into my ears; another bolt struck me, then one on my nose. "Open your mouth," He said, and He touched my tongue, searing as a coal from the altar.[16] "Lift your hands," He continued. Lightning shot into my fingers and palms. He placed His hands on my shoulders, and then He crossed His hands and laid them on my shoulders again.[17] He moved to my heart and diaphragm, my thighs and knees; then God stooped over and placed His hands on my feet.[18] Power shot into them like nails.

## The Sword Not of Man

"I AM GIVING into your hand this day the sword not of man.[19] This sword is two-edged. It can bar or open the way to the tree of life." He spoke to someone near. "Bring the sheath to her."

A large, powerful angel knelt and gave the sheath into the light surrounding the throne. Two cherubs were on either side of the angel. These cherubs must have been over eight feet tall. Each had two faces. One cherub had the face of a man in front and a lion in back. The other had the face of an eagle in front and of an ox in back.[20] Each had two wings with hands under their wings. Their legs were straight like a man's but ended in hooves. Taupe-colored feathers covered their bodies like fish-scale mail. They were full of eyes around their bodies and within their wings. I had seen no celestial beings that held such terror as well as majesty.

"Step forward," my Father said. "Let Me buckle this on you." The scabbard was very fine, pure gold and hung on the left side. "Now, the sword," He said.

From the Light that is my Father came the most beautiful sword. It appeared to have a blade of white gold or diamond with a golden handle that was jeweled. I could see through it. It was all light and fire, and it hovered in the air. Jesus stepped forward, and He and my Father put their hands on it. It glowed even brighter. It was as though lightning and thunder or an explosion went off within it. They then removed their hands, and a beautiful sound of music or singing came from it.

"Grasp it," my Father said.

"Anna," Jesus said, "let Me help you." He came to my right side and put His hand on mine; together we reached for the sword. It leaped into my hand. Jesus smiled at me. "You may wield this sword because we are one.[21] This sword is sheathed on the outside, but it is also hidden within for the hand and the mouth."[22]

Suddenly, the sword became a red quill pen and an inkwell full of golden ink.[23] Jesus continued, "The Holy Spirit writes for the Father. The Holy Spirit is ever proceeding, never initiating, Anna."[24] Pure, pure water with flicks of fire in it began to flow from the pen. "He writes for Me and for the sake of the kingdom." The pen and inkwell changed back into the sword. Jesus continued, "With the sword not of man, chains will be cut asunder and yokes of iron severed."[25]

## Jachin and Boaz

MY FATHER SPOKE. "Jachin and Boaz will go with you now," He said, referring to the two cherubs.[26] "They guard the sword.[27] They are very powerful and most loving; they will be your friends." He addressed the cherubim, "Guard well." They bowed and then turned around and bowed again. Their bodies had two fronts and no backs. Then my Father spoke again, "Now, Anna, the mantle."

## The Installation

### The Mantle

FROM THE LEFT side of the Father, where the Holy Spirit had spoken, came forth a shimmering mantle that hovered in midair. Jachin and Boaz moved over to stand on either side of it. The mantle was both visible and invisible, like a gossamer, with thousands of lights within it. The material was like breath, but breath that was full of living light.

"The mantle that you are to wear," my Father said, indicating the cloak.

### The Whirlwind

I SLID THE sword into its sheath in order to put on the cloak. I expected Jachin and Boaz to help me, but instead, a huge whirlwind stirred before the throne.[28] The garment swirled up into the whirlwind. The angels aloft joined with it by flying within the whirlwind, around and around.

"The Holy Spirit bestows His own mantle," my Father said.

As the cloak began to come down, there was lightning within it. Light changed and pulsated around it, and the Holy Spirit began to proclaim through the singing of the angels:

### The Holy Spirit's Song

Let the brush of angels' wings
Never blind the eyes
Of those who see beyond the veil
To gaze at paradise.
Gaze on, gaze on past the golden rim,
Gaze on past streets of gold,
Gaze on past all created things
To the new One, ever old.

Ever old and ever new,
Ancient of Days is He.

Infinity within His hands,
Light eternally.
Compassionate God, He who is good,
Compassionate God of might,
Life as a river flows from Your throne
To those who turn from night.

Let the cherubim in awe,
The seraphim in praise,
As those who see beyond the veil,
Upon Him ever gaze.
Gaze on, gaze on past the golden rim,
Gaze on past streets of gold,
Gaze on past all created things
To the new One, ever old.

As the mantle neared the sea of glass, what seemed to be electricity was popping and arcing within the cloak; colors were rippling within it like the changing colors of a certain type of jellyfish in the ocean. The two cherubs stepped to the side to make room for the mantle. It was suspended in midair in front of me.

"What do I do?" I asked.

"Wait, Anna," my Father said.

There was silence in heaven.[29] It was as though everything held its breath. Everyone in the throne room was silent. Gradually, with a gentle, pleasant breeze, the garment moved toward me. I held out my arms as if someone were going to help me put on a coat. The mantle was shimmering. It was like breath. As I slipped into it, however, I realized that I became transparent, invisible in certain areas. The only parts of me that could be seen were my hands, my feet, and my head.[30]

Before I could think about this further, Jesus said to me, "Anna, take these."

"What are they?" I asked.

# The Installation

## The Shoes

"SHOES OF PORPOISE," He said.[31] I felt this was a play on the word "purpose," but I did not know why.[32]

I looked at them. They too were gossamer. They laced up the front like high-top work shoes that covered the ankle, but there were no soles in the shoes. "They have no soles," I said.

Jesus smiled, "No, the Godhead is to be the expression of the soul."[33] (He seemed to enjoy His pun.) "These shoes keep your feet naked, touching the holy ground above, but leave you unjustified before mankind.[34-35] You will be invisible to man but intimate with God. These cover the ankle and the heel also. Invisibility will work the cross in your life to the point that there will be no exposed heel nor any strength in the natural man displayed."[36-38]

I sat on the sea of glass to put them on. "These are the strangest shoes I have ever seen," I said.

"Yes," Jesus answered. "Few want to wear them. They are out of style."

"Will they stay on?" I laughed.

"Yes, unless you yourself take them off. You can expose your walk before mankind, but there will be no life in it.[39] The worm of death will crawl in and out of that exposure, Anna."[40] Then He asked, "Can you walk in the fire of invisibility that mankind will not give you glory? Few alive today will wear these shoes, for they want their glory from mankind instead of God."[41]

I finished lacing the shoes and stood. The tops of my feet were invisible. "Lord," I asked seriously, "am I going to be able to do this?"

"No," He smiled, "but I will, if you will let Me."[42]

I searched His face. "I believe," I said softly. "Help my unbelief."[43]

## A Burning Flame of Love

SUDDENLY, THE THRONE became a towering column of fire,

roaring louder than any forge on earth.[44] I involuntarily stepped backward, for the fire seemed hotter than the furnaces that melt iron ore into molten magma.

"Anna," my Father said with a voice of thunder, "can you live within the fire?"[45-46]

"Father," I said hesitantly, "I cannot wish for painful experiences, but I can wish for You. Give me the grace to desire You more than life itself."

Huge hands of fire reached out to me. "Come," He said.

With a big gulp, I began to move forward slowly.

Jesus took my hand. "I will go with you," He said gravely.

Suddenly, when Jesus took my hand, my yearning for my Father grew more intense. I began crying out in my desire for more of Him: "Daddy, Daddy, Daddy, Daddy!" As I began to call to Him, it was as though God opened Himself with a great, silent cry or hunger on His part to have me closer also. It was as though we were instantly sucked into Him.[47]

We were standing amid coals that were white from the intense heat.[48] I too began to heat up. The light was so bright that I could barely see Jesus for the glory within the blazing, white haze.

## Fiery Comets

THEN FIRE RESEMBLING great, flaming comets began to hit me from all sides. Two hit my eyes, and my eyes burst into flame.[49] As these fiery missiles assailed me, my Father began to speak, "The fire of My holiness, the fire of My love, the fire of My compassion, the fire of My wisdom, the fire of My understanding, the fire of My knowledge, the fire of My zeal, the fire of My purity, the fire of My mercy . . ."[50]

My fingers went to my burning lips. "Prudence," He said. "Breathe in."[51] I sucked in fire. Fire now was outside and inside of me.

# The Installation

## The Beautiful and Terrible Eyes

IN THE MIDST of the coals of fire, I saw two huge eyes aflame: beautiful, terrible beyond description. The eyes looked at me. I could not turn my own eyes away; they were so awesome in both beauty and dreadful wonder.[52]

"Your eyes are beautiful," I said. "I wish to see as You see."

"Fix your gaze upon Me," He said, and His eyes came into mine and then back again. I continued to look and burn until I felt as though my eyes were burned out of their sockets.

He spoke, "Let Me look through your eyes.[53] Let My heart look with mercy upon My children and upon the lost.[54] Let My lips speak."[55]

Passionate, all-consuming love welled up within me. "Make me a burning flame of love for You," I cried from the depths of my being.

## The Lord in His Glory

SUDDENLY JESUS WAS standing directly in front of me within the coals of fire. Brilliant, white light was coming from Him; tongues of fire radiated out from Him at intervals. His eyes were aflame also. He spoke, "As My heart is represented by the garden in Paradise, each believer's heart is likewise represented as a locked garden wherein we meet. The Father's heart is represented by these coals of fire, aflame with love.[56] The heart of our Father is pure, aflame, and holy. You must be invited to walk amid the coals of fire, for although our Father loves all, not all are invited within.[57] For those whom He invites, complete oneness is the only thing that will satisfy: consuming and being consumed, where all sin is unthinkable and painful in the extreme. Like a moth to a flame, one is drawn closer and closer into holiness. Any thought of darkness that hinders perfect union with Light—any wavering in obedience, any thought that is not love—becomes painful; for to that degree, the perfect oneness with the Father is disturbed. Love desires more and more of the Beloved. There is pain in separation.

Darkness causes blockages, but love seeks more and more of the Light—more, ever more, until the child also is a walking flame of love in constant communion with Love Himself.

"My heart yearns in ever increasing multiplications for My Father. His love consumes Me, and I hunger and thirst for more.[58]

"Let this desire so be in you—that His goodness draws forth thankfulness and praise, that His mercy draws forth adoration, that His holiness draws forth worship, that like a true child of the Father, Love begets love and trust."

With that, He took my hand and led me out of the coals of fire.

# The Return

J ESUS LED ME back to the great assembly. As we emerged, my Father stood and proclaimed, "Let it be recorded. She has passed through the coals of fire; My name is on her forehead. She is My chancellor." He placed His hands on my shoulders and turned me around to face those on the sea of glass.

"I accept this responsibility," I said.

"So be it," He said.

Then all of heaven broke into high praises of God for His faithfulness—music and choirs, fragrances and colors, with angels beyond number bowing before Him who sits on the throne. Joy abounded.

Quietly I told Jesus that I was not sure of all that my new duties entailed.

He leaned over and whispered, "Write what you have seen and heard."

"Oh," I nodded.

A lively circle dance began, and the angels came down from their stations above and joined in the circles with the redeemed: *mahanaim.*[1]

As I stood there, two angels brushed me off with their wings, for I was covered with ashes.[2] I felt a bit fuzzy also, as though I had gone through something and had not recovered or stabilized. My eyes felt stretched.

## The Gift of a Venerable Angel

WHILE THE CELEBRATION continued, my Father spoke to me privately. "Anna," He said. Jesus and I turned to face Him. "I have a gift for you."

A large, old-looking angel came to stand beside me. He seemed slightly blue because of the blue light emanating from him. He had a partially bald head and a very long white beard. He wore a full-length, sleeveless mantle woven with various shades of blue. Underneath was an even deeper blue robe. Light flashed within the cloak.

"This is a friend of Mine, Anna," Jesus said to me.[3] "He has come to train you."

My Father said, "Elijah is a gift from My hand. He is beloved of Me and revered among the angels. He will be with you now during your journey on earth." He said to the angel, "Elijah."

Elijah knelt before the Father.

"Will you help to train My daughter?" my Father asked.

"I will," Elijah replied.

"My friend," Jesus said. Jesus took Elijah by the hand, raised him to his feet, and He kissed both of the angel's cheeks. "This is my Anna, Elijah," Jesus said. "She is beloved of Me."

"Hello, Anna," the angel said and took my right hand into

his hands. "I am honored to be of assistance," he said. "It is my desire to serve the great and living God."

"Thank you," I said. "I hope to be a good student."

## The Father's Exhortation

"ANNA," MY FATHER continued, "My people wait for the hope that will seal My covenant of peace. Are you ready?"

"Yes, Daddy."

"Well then, My Anna," He said, "let us bring them into the throne room and into My heart."

His glory came from Him and kissed my forehead.[4]

Jesus leaned over and kissed my hand. "I am with you," He said, looking deeply into my eyes.

"Thank you," I smiled, continuing to gaze at Him whom my heart adores.

He squeezed my hand.

## Departure

THEN ELIJAH AND I bowed and turned to leave. Before we reached the area where the dancing was taking place, I turned again to look at my Father. The mercy, splendor, and faithfulness of our God overwhelmed me. I choked a little as I said, "I love You, Daddy."

"I love you, Anna," my Father replied.

I smiled again and began to walk from the throne room with Elijah. Epaggelias followed right behind us, and Jachin and Boaz dropped in behind him and slightly to either side.

As we walked through the dancers, the redeemed acknowledged our passing. Their looks were warm. I was as comfortable as being among loved ones on earth and more so. *What a family,* I thought to myself. *What friends.*

Clara waved to me from among those dancing. I looked for other angels that I knew now, but there were so many of them circling around that it was difficult to distinguish quickly one face from another.

## On the Path

ALMOST IMMEDIATELY WE were walking on the path in Paradise.

"Another promise kept," Epaggelias said, speaking aloud to himself.[5]

I turned my head to look at him.

He chuckled to himself, "My, He is faithful."

Jachin and Boaz showed respect for the depth of Epaggelias' gratitude. They nodded solemnly.

## Questioning Elijah

"ELIJAH," I SAID.

He looked at me.

"Why did the Lord give me a new name?"

Elijah answered, "Because you are new. Your mission, your call, your direction on earth have changed. You are called now to reveal the Father's heart, and I am to be of assistance to you in doing this. So few understand, Anna, but they long to understand.

"The world is too much with the children of God. It is as though the earth, from which their frames are made, has too much of a hold upon them. Truly their vessels of clay should not dictate the course of the lives of the redeemed, but they seem to have difficulty separating the vessel from that which the vessel contains—seepage. It is as though their clay is still wet and has seeped into their souls.

"However, this manner of life will no longer suffice. The times are coming and now are already here when the separation between soul and spirit, between body and soul, together with cleanness of heart, must take place for survival.[6–8]

"Anna, there is a spirit in the land that distracts continually from the true.[9] Because of this, our God is sending again the spirit of Elijah.

"The greatest need is still to know the Father. He must reveal Himself in greater measure before the end of these times. I have come to help reveal the heart of the Father to the children, for His heart is for them, and to prick their hearts to seek Him in order that they might know Him. The Father has brought you forth at this time to be one" (I felt that "among many" was implied) "to reveal His heart.

"When the spirit of Elijah is in the land, there are judgments, droughts, and visible confrontations with the enemies of God. As it was with those who worshiped Baal, always there will be violent confrontations and great exhibitions of God's power; but first, Anna, the Father's children must have a greater certainty of His love.[10] They must be rooted and grounded in Christ, empowered by the Holy Spirit, and their eyes looking above and fixed on Him.

"You will enjoy revealing the Father's heart, and I will enjoy assisting you."

## The Dark Cloud

I ASKED, "WHAT is the dark cloud about which my Father spoke, Elijah?"

He replied, "The dark cloud that surrounds God is actually the dense oil of the Spirit, a great good, a visible sign of the magnitude of the anointing, incomprehensible to mankind and therefore seemingly dark.[11] To the majority of mankind, He is hidden in darkness. Light that they cannot see emanates from Him. To many of His children He seems hidden, but the fire of His love is burning through the density of that oil now and will allow His children to see His love, His mercy, and His fatherly compassion, as well as the startling reality of His holiness.

"This fire will burn all that is wood, hay, and stubble in the lives of His children. They must desire the fire and long for His holiness. His heart is turned toward them, and the fire of His love will reveal this. The hearts of the children will long to turn toward Him, to walk through the fire of purification, and to rest in His arms. As the enemy hates the fire, so must God's children love it, for in and through the fire, they will see God."

## At the Stairport

WE HAD ARRIVED at the stairport. Elijah smiled at me, "Are you ready to go to work?"

"Yes," I smiled in return. I took his hand in mine. "Thank you, Elijah, and all of you," I said, turning to Epaggelias, Jachin, and Boaz. "Thank you. I bless you in the name of the Lord Jesus."

"Thank you, Anna," they replied together. "We receive that." We stood there awkwardly.

"Now what do I do?" I asked.

"You return," Elijah chuckled.

"And what about you?" I asked.

All four faces of Jachin and Boaz said, "We go with you, Anna. Remember?"

"Oh," I said perplexed, "right."

I turned to walk toward the docking station, and they disappeared, though I knew they were with me.

## Azar Reappears

AZAR APPEARED, LEANING on the docking post. "Ah, here you are—well, parts of you anyway," he smiled, referring to my visible head and hands.

I looked down at my cloak and shoes. I could see right through them to the path.

He began to remove the red cord from the post. "And your Father has revealed to you the reason you came?" he grinned broadly.

"Yes," I smiled, and then the wonder and mystery of it all swept over me. "Yes," I repeated with a greater sense of awe.

"Are you ready to return then?" he continued, trying to help me gather my scattered focus.

"Oh, yes," I said, suddenly realizing that I needed to concentrate on the task before me. I moved toward the stairs.

"Remember not to look down over the sides of the stairs when going back. It takes a little getting used to, but we need to learn sometime, don't we?" He sounded ever so like a nanny.

He began to let down the stairs.

"Thank you for your help, Azar."

"That's my name," he chirped. "Still I hope we don't see each other too often. Naw, just kidding," he said. "If you slip on the steps, I'll steady you."

I laughed at him, shaking my head.

"Give me your hand," he said, leading me to the top of the stairs. "Now be careful with the first step. Light isn't slippery, but it does have a different feel from materials on earth, you know."

He held my hand until I had taken the first step and then the next.

"All right!" he cheered, and began whistling through his teeth and clapping loudly as one would at a sport's event. "Take care, luv."

## The Descent

I COULD NOT help but smile, even while steadying myself on the stairs. As I began to descend, he called after me, "Remember the stairports are all over the world and ready for your use."

"Thank you," I called back to him loudly; I lifted my hand without looking back. I could sense that he was watching me the full length of the stairs. He continued to hold the end of the cord.

When I reached the bottom, I turned and waved, although he was only a speck. The cord tightened; the stairs in its first stage retracted, then the second, then the third, and disappeared.

## On Earth Again

I WAS BACK at the location from which I had escaped. Far away in the distance, I could hear the sound of a fierce battle in progress. Quickly I clawed my way to the top of the sandy hill again. I wanted to see if any of the city remained after the battering ram's attack.

Where the walled city had stood, now there was only debris, scattered stones, and pockets of burning. Still I knew that the stones, the living stones of Christ's true church, were safe. They may have climbed some stairway, or hidden in caves, or floated on the water; but the living stones had survived.

I stood there a moment looking at the devastation before me. Then I looked up, cocked my head to one side, and smiled. "Reporting for work, Daddy."

# Afterword

# How It Happened

"YOU WILL RECEIVE a visitation." With these simple words our lives were blasted from one realm into another, although we did not realize it at the time.

My husband and I received this promise at a dinner party a few days before we left the city. Four years before, the Lord had brought us to that large metropolitan area after my husband's retirement from the pastoral ministry. We brought together pastors and intercessors—crossing denominational lines—in a citywide prayer movement.

After the Lord raised up leadership from among the pastors we turned the prayer ministry of the city over to them. At our last citywide gathering with the ministers, they laid hands on us, blessed us, and sent us out to serve the larger body of Christ.

"You will be in a cabin at the season of Hanukkah when you receive this visitation," the dinner guest had continued. He was a friend of ours who had an internationally recognized prophetic ministry. Although we had known him for several years, he had never spoken words from the Lord to us personally.

I had seen angels intermittently while we were in the city and had even seen the Lord several times from a distance, but a visitation was far beyond anything my husband or I had ever experienced. To say the least, we were skeptical.

However, our God is merciful as well as full of surprises.

On the eve of Hanukkah, 1994, in a cabin on a lake in Texas, suddenly, the heavens opened as the Spirit ushered me into the very throne room of God. I saw with such startling clarity that I could not deny what I was seeing. Everything I saw and heard was different from what I had thought: more extra-ordinary, yet comfortable. It seemed as though I were at home.

I began to visit heaven on a daily basis. Although at first the visits were tiring, I was careful to journal them. I do not think of these visits as visions, for I believe that what I saw is actu-ally there. John told of such an experience in Revelation 4:1. John reported what he saw and heard when he was summoned to heaven in the Spirit.

There were visions also. This book begins with a vision. Visions seem to be a pictorial language—visual aids repre-senting truth from God in which one may or may not participate. One example of the visions given to John while he was in heaven is Revelation 9:17.

When I shared these revelations with my husband, the Lord allowed my husband to experience what I was experiencing by being there.

Then on January 1, 1997, the Lord asked us to compile a book from some of the early revelations and to include an addendum containing scriptural verification and illumination concerning all that was seen and heard. He asked us to complete the entire manuscript in one year.

# Afterword

This book is in response to the Lord's request. My husband and I can truly say that we do not believe this book is our own. We have never served the Lord in any way that has been so completely Him. Everything in this book is true. If there are errors in the way things are described, the errors are entirely our doing.

All those who are born again in Christ Jesus sit with Him, in spirit, in heavenly places. However, He has been gracious to allow some of us to see into that realm, according to His Word in John 1:51.

Moreover, we found that these revelations were not for the two of us alone, as we had first thought, but for the body of Christ, of which we are members.

We, who are bondservants of Christ, bless you in His name.

—ANNA ROUNTREE

*This extensive notes section provides the scriptural support*
*for the revelations that have been presented in this book.*
*These scriptures—with their accompanying explanatory*
*text—give a wonderful foundational understanding*
*of the believer's future.*
*—The Publisher*

# Notes

## Chapter 1
### The Attack

1. God's judgment against sin has begun with His household, the church (1 Pet. 4:17; Rev. 14:7). The battering ram with the iron head of a goat (Lev. 17:7; 2 Chron. 11:15, "satyrs") symbolizes the satanic attack that God permits to come against the false church in the spiritual wilderness (Rev. 17:3–5). He did the same thing to apostate Jerusalem (Ezek. 21:21–27; Rev. 18:8). His purpose is to separate the weeds from the wheat of the living and true church (Matt. 13:40–43; 1 Cor. 11:18–19; Rev. 18:2, 4).

   The king of Babylon in the Ezekiel passage above represents Satan, who was the power behind the throne of the earthly king of Babylon, even as Satan was in the case of the king of Tyre (Ezek. 28:2, 12).

2. In the last days before the Lord Jesus returns, the false church will be in league with the Antichrist, who is called "a scarlet beast, full of blasphemous names" (Rev. 17:3; 13:1), and who is the personification of Satan, the "great red dragon" (Rev. 12:3). The Antichrist and his armies will turn upon this whorish church and destroy her by fire (Rev. 17:16).

3. The man-controlled organization that calls herself "the church" is centered upon the things of this world and seems oblivious to any impending judgment of God against her. This also was the case with the people in the days of Noah and in the city of Sodom (Luke 17:26–30). This church will not understand what God is doing (Matt. 24:39).

4. The false church is called "Babylon the Great" (Rev. 17:5) because she is the final form of the satanically inspired, religious system that began in the days of the tyrant Nimrod to exalt herself through witchcraft and idolatry (Gen. 10:8–10; 11:1–4). This first Babylonish church used bricks instead of stone to build her city, even as today's Babylonish church builds herself up with man-made materials,

instead of relying upon Jesus Christ to build her with living stones (Matt. 16:18; 1 Pet. 2:5). The adobe walls represent that which is constructed by "the flesh" of religious people whom God calls "dust" (Gen. 3:19; Jer. 17:5) and who are powerless against Satan and his hordes (2 Cor. 10:3–4; Isa. 31:1).

5. In Genesis 28:12–13, Jacob dreamed that "a ladder was set on the earth with its top reaching to heaven" with the angels of God ascending and descending on it. The Lord, in His preincarnate form, was standing above it.

   Jesus Christ is the ladder or "the way" into heaven, for "no one comes to the Father but through [Him]" (John 14:6). He told the first disciples that they would see the heavens opened and the angels ascending and descending upon Him (John 1:51).

6. The scarlet cord that is secured to the first section of the stairway into heaven represents the first stage of redemption through the cross of Calvary (Josh. 2:18). This is the shed blood of Christ that releases us from guilt and separation from God that was caused by our sins (Rev. 1:5). The way is now open to the throne of God by faith (Heb. 10:22) through hope (Heb. 7:19) in the Lord Jesus.

7. The second section of the stairway is the second stage of redemption through the cross of Calvary. It is the release from the power of sin by the death of the totally corrupt corporate spiritual heart of the human race. This happened when the old human race died with Christ on Calvary. God gives those who would believe in His Son a new heart that lives by the resurrection life of the Lord (Eph. 2:10; Rom. 6:6–8; 2 Cor. 5:14–17; Col. 3:3; Gal. 2:20).

8. The third section secures one's position in the heavenly realm with Christ "far above all rule and authority and power and dominion" of the enemy (Eph. 1:21). It is to live in God (Col. 3:3) the heavenly life of love, ministering to His needs (Ps. 65:4; Rev. 3:12). It is the place of the disciple who continually bears about in his body the sentence of death from the same, inner cross to his own self-expression that Jesus bore daily here on the earth (2 Cor. 4:10; 2 Cor. 1:9; Matt. 16:24; Phil. 2:7). It is the final stage of overcoming the enemies of God, where the soul life (mind, emotions, and will) of Christ Jesus is being imparted to the believer (Matt. 16:25). It is the place of the overcoming Christian in every generation (Rev. 2:7, 11, 17, 26–28; 3:5, 12, 21). The disciple who overcomes the world, the flesh, and the devil as the Lord Jesus overcame them seeks only the living God, in comparison with whom all things are as rubbish (Rev. 3:21; Col. 3:1; Phil. 3:8).

# Notes

9. The area where one arrives first when entering heaven is called Paradise. One then moves on to the celestial city—the heavenly Jerusalem—and finally to the throne of God the Father (Heb. 12:22–23). Jesus promised the repentant thief whom they crucified with Him at Calvary that He would meet him in Paradise that very day (Luke 23:43).

   The word *Paradise* means "park or garden." The Father designed the true Garden of Eden there especially for the Lord Jesus (Song of Sol. 5:1; 6:2; Ezek. 28:13). In His garden the original tree of life still grows (Rev. 2:7).

10. Slaves did not wear shoes in households in biblical days; only the members of the family were shod (Luke 15:22). Hence, removing one's shoes in the presence of God acknowledged that one did not own or control the holy ground on which one stood (Exod. 3:5; Josh. 5:15).

11. The living church is able to climb into Paradise in spirit and to live "hidden with Christ in God" in spirit and heart (1 Pet. 3:4; Col. 3:3) as described in the three sections of the stairway of Christ under notes 6, 7, and 8 above (John 3:21; Isa. 26:12; Ps. 31:19–20). His people also are able to: (a) hide in caves in places prepared by God (Rev. 12:14), as did David and his men (1 Sam. 22:1); or (b) float on the water, as did Noah and his household during the flood (Gen. 7:23).

    The living church on earth is the body of born-again Christians who share a common life of glorifying and obeying the Lord Jesus through keeping His Word and through worship, prayer, and fellowship—all as energized by the Holy Spirit.

    Christians are those who have been born again by the Holy Spirit implanting the Word of Scripture concerning salvation within their new hearts and spirits so that they have begun to experience the life, light, and love of God.

12. In heaven whatever one asks for immediately appears because the abiding fruit of Christ's character is in everyone; all things are available in Him, as He promised (John 15:16).

13. The garden of God in heaven (Ezek. 28:13), which is the pattern for the Garden of Eden that was on the earth (Gen. 2:8–9), contains fruit trees, too. The heavenly fruit is made of God's light and is eaten by the angels and the redeemed there (Rev. 2:7).

14. Every created object and every living creation (angelic, human, animal, plant) in heaven is formed of God's light, which is substantial and can be felt and allows the divine light of the glory of God to shine

through everything (Rev. 21:23; 22:5). There are no shadows there, no hint of darkness.

15. The Hebrew word that means "help" is *azar.* The work of certain angels is that of rescuing believers from danger as described in Psalm 91:11–12: God gives "His angels charge concerning you, to guard you in all your ways. They will bear you up in their hands, lest you strike your foot against a stone." An angel of help rescued Daniel from the lions (Dan. 6:22) and Peter from jail (Acts 12:11).

16. Angels only know what God the Spirit reveals to them. There are matters that Christians know but that angels do not know (1 Pet. 1:12).

# Chapter 2
## Sandcastles

1. The angel told Moses to take off his sandals because the presence of
   the angel of the Lord in the burning bush made the soil there holy
   (Exod. 3:5). In heaven no one wears shoes, for all the ground there is
   holy to God (Dan. 10:6; Rev. 1:15). The priests who ministered in the
   tabernacle wore no shoes (Exod. 30:18–20).

   Slaves went barefooted (Luke 15:22), but Christians are bond-
   slaves who have freely chosen to serve their Lord and Master forever
   out of love for Him (Exod. 21:2–6; Rev. 22:3).

2. The Hebrew and the Greek words usually translated "messenger" are
   also translated "angel." Angels from heaven not only carry messages,
   as did Gabriel to the virgin Mary (Luke 1:26ff), but they may also fulfill a special mission or represent God in some manner. All angels
   who are sent from heaven for a particular task or who are assigned to
   accompany individual believers on earth "render service for the sake
   of those who will inherit salvation" (Heb. 1:14).

3. The first mention of the word angel in the Bible is Genesis 16:7,
   when "the angel of the LORD" brought God's promise concerning His
   multiplying of Hagar's descendants through Ishmael, her son (Gen.
   16:10). This is the first of many recorded promises delivered by
   angels to people on earth. "The angel of the LORD" often speaks and
   acts throughout the Bible for God (Gen. 22:15–18) and at times as
   God (Exod. 3:2, 4, 6).

   God always keeps His promises (Josh. 21:45). When the Bible
   says that God "remembered His covenant" promises (Exod. 2:24), it
   does not mean that He had forgotten; it means that He was now going
   to carry forward their fulfillment in a particular situation.

4. Angels often know the thoughts of others without them needing to
   speak (Gen. 21:17). In heaven also one often knows the answer as
   soon as one asks a question. This is true because there is no sin or
   "flesh" there to hinder the flow of knowledge to one instantly by the
   Holy Spirit, for one's spirit is fully open to the Spirit, from whom
   nothing is hidden (1 Cor. 2:10–11; Heb. 4:13). Paul speaks of this in 1
   Corinthians 13:12: "Now I know [on earth] in part, but then [in
   heaven] I shall know fully just as I also have been fully known."

5. Jesus did not do many miracles for the people in His hometown of Nazareth "because of their unbelief" (Matt. 13:58). But the promises of God to the Jews will be fulfilled, for the unbelief of some people of that nation "will not nullify the faithfulness of God" (Rom. 3:3; 9:27; 11:23–24).

6. Job, Daniel, and King Nebuchadnezzar all called God the revealer of mysteries (Job 12:22; Dan. 2:28, 47). Mysteries are hidden truths known by God but unknown by others until God reveals them (Matt. 13:11; 1 Cor. 2:9–12).

7. Jesus said that "the Scriptures...bear witness" of Him (John 5:39), for He is the key that opens the Scriptures (Luke 24:32). To the two disciples on the road to Emmaus, Jesus "explained...the things concerning Himself in all the Scriptures" (Luke 24:27). He also "opened [the] minds [of those gathered in Jerusalem that same day] to understand the Scriptures" by telling them "that all things which are written about [Him] in the law of Moses and the Prophets and the Psalms must be fulfilled" (Luke 24:45, 44). "The Scripture cannot be broken" (John 10:35) and "stands forever" (Isa. 40:8; Ps. 119:89). God has magnified His Word according to all His name (Ps. 138:2).

8. Every firstborn Hebrew male was redeemed in order for him to be allowed to continue living—at the redemption price of five (the number that signifies grace) shekels of silver (Num. 18:15–16; Exod. 13:15). Therefore silver is a type of redemption from death through Jesus Christ. The tour guide made no charge to the people taking the tour, for the full price has been paid by Jesus on the cross. All now is by grace through the blood of the Lamb of God (1 Pet. 1:13, 18–19; 2 Cor. 9:8).

9. In the Garden of Eden on earth, one river flowed out to water the garden (Gen. 2:10). This river was the physical representation of the one spiritual "river of the water of life, clear as crystal" that waters all of heaven, flowing from the throne of God and of the Lamb (Rev. 22:1). The heavenly river of life is a picture of the flow of unending life by the Holy Spirit to every being and everything there.

   Even now God grants to His faithful children on earth to "drink of the river of [His] delights. For with [Him] is the fountain of life" (Ps. 36:8–9) that will flow out through them to others (John 7:37–39).

10. Flowers in heaven and on earth represent revelations of the beauty of God (Song of Sol. 1:14; 2:1; 5:13). But the true flowers in heaven are everlasting and perfect in their form, beauty, and fragrance (Heb.

9:24; James 1:17). Because flowers in heaven are made from the light of God, and because they, with all of heaven, obey God fully, they return to their original shape after being trampled (Ps. 103:21–22; 148:1, 5–6).

11. Angels who minister to particular believers on earth (Heb. 1:14) often have names that identify each one's function. The angel Crystal Clear is so named because the Lord teaches the truth through her in very easily perceived and unmistakable terms. All heaven is formed of supernatural light that is substantial and transparent, reflecting the glory of God in everything everywhere (Ps. 8:1; Rev. 5:13).

12. There is no sea in heaven or on the new earth (Rev. 21:1), because the sea represents rebellion that cannot bring life but issues in death. The unbelieving peoples of the earth are often represented by "the tossing sea, for it cannot be quiet, and its waters toss up refuse and mud" (Isa. 57:20–21; Jude 13).

13. Jesus taught the lesson about building on sand in Matthew 7:24–27. His words are "spirit and are life" (John 6:63) to those who act upon them by building upon Christ the Rock as the foundation. But those who put their hope in anything that is built on the sands of earth will see it all swept away one day (2 Pet. 3:10).

14. "The world" is one meaning of the Greek word *cosmos,* which is used in the New Testament to denote the spiritual kingdom of Satan on the earth that is ruled by aggression, deception, lust, greed, murder, and pride (1 John 2:15–17; John 8:44; Rev. 12:9). All human beings are born into that kingdom with the spirit of evil working in them (Eph. 2:1–3). The only way to leave that kingdom of darkness is to be born again by the Holy Spirit into Jesus Christ (1 Cor. 1:30) and so be transferred out of this "world" and into His kingdom (Col. 1:13).

15. The "flesh" is one meaning of the Greek word *sarx* to denote the independent use of the earthly, outer person of soul and body. The law of sin in the members of the human body (Rom. 7:23) has also corrupted all natural expression of the faculties of the soul (mind, emotions, and will). This expression is called the old self (Eph. 4:22), and "nothing good dwells in...my flesh" (Rom. 7:18). The only good we have in us as believers is Christ Jesus (Luke 18:19; John 15:5).

16. The copper in a penny gives it a sour taste in the mouth. Copper in the Scriptures signifies the righteous judgment of God against sin. The altar for animal sacrifice in the courtyard of the wilderness tabernacle

was plated with a copper alloy, probably bronze (Exod. 27:1–2; Num. 21:6, 8–9).

17. The angel Crystal Clear imparts a powerful and refreshing blessing because the light from God flows through her hands. The angel Gabriel touched Daniel and revived him (Dan. 8:18), and later another angel came to strengthen him (Dan. 10:10, 16, 18).

# Chapter 3

## Angels in Training

1. For believers to grow up into Christ in the new self (Col. 3:10; 2 Cor. 4:16; Eph. 4:15) and be joined as one spirit to the spirit of Jesus (1 Cor. 6:17), the Holy Spirit must train them to rely upon the Lord's life of complete obedience (Heb. 2:10; 5:8–9) that is available to fill each believer minute by minute (Eph. 5:18; Col. 3:17; 2 Cor. 3:5–6).

2. All growth in the natural and in the spiritual is from God (1 Cor. 3:7; Acts 17:25). The angelic host of heaven was created through Christ and for Him, as were all things on the earth (Col. 1:16). Therefore as the redeemed on earth are to grow up in all aspects into the Lord Jesus, including the experiential knowledge of Him (2 Pet. 3:18; Eph. 4:15), so the heavenly beings are to grow in the knowledge of God both through relationship to Christ Jesus (Col. 2:2–3) and through revelation by the Holy Spirit (Rev. 7:14).

3. Toil in working is the result of sin (Gen. 3:17–19). God rests in the midst of His working (Heb. 4:10; John 5:17), and so do the heavenly host, because the Father has handed over all things to the Son (Luke 10:22) who gives rest to the angels and to the redeemed as they work with Him in union and trustful obedience (Matt. 11:28–30; Heb. 3:18–19).

   It is not their particular duty or gifting that dominates the hearts of the angels but rather their desire to serve and know God more and more (Ps. 103:20–21).

4. When God grants visions of heaven to believers, at times He opens their eyes to see many angels and/or the redeemed gathered together (Rev. 5:11; 7:9). At other times He allows only one or a few to be seen (Rev. 10; 15:5–6).

5. There are examples in Scripture of the private tutoring of individuals through visions of God and of heaven: Moses (Exod. 33:11), Ezekiel (Ezek. 1; 2:7–8), and John in the Book of Revelation.

6. In heaven, in the presence of God, one's heart is satisfied, and one's spirit is filled with the light of God. This enables a person to know intuitively in a way similar to how God knows (1 Cor. 13:12), and

there is no awareness of the need to ask questions. The disciples had a foretaste of this in John 21:12, after Jesus rose from the dead.

7. The culmination of any vision of heaven would be to hear the Father speak. John in the first twenty chapters of the Book of Revelation saw many things occurring and that were to occur in heaven. It was only in verse 5 of chapter 21 that God the Father spoke to him from the throne.

8. God does not override the measure of free will that He has carefully preserved in each person (Deut. 30:19; Josh. 24:15; Job 34:4). He desires our willing consent; very often Jesus said that if anyone wishes to come... let him (Matt. 16:24; 19:21; 20:26–27; John 7:37).

9. Distance in the spiritual realm does not present a problem as it does on the earth. John says that immediately after Jesus spoke to him to come up to heaven, he was there in the throne room of God (Rev. 4:1–2). The hand of God also caught Ezekiel by a lock of his head, lifted him up between earth and heaven, and brought him to Jerusalem (Ezek. 8:3). The Holy Spirit also whisked Philip from the wilderness to Azotus (or Ashdod) some twenty miles away (Acts 8:39–40).

10. The red cross worn on the arms of the healing angels signifies the ministry of healing through Jesus Christ that He began on earth as a foretaste of the coming redemption through His blood sacrifice (Isa. 53:4–5; 1 Pet. 2:24). By the shedding of His precious blood on Calvary, He made atonement for sins and thereby destroyed the power of the works of the devil in causing sickness and death (Matt. 8:16; Acts 10:38; 1 John 3:8; Heb. 2:14).

    The Lord continues His ministry of healing from heaven as the Holy Spirit makes effectual Christ's triumph on the cross over the enemies of God (Col. 2:15). Believers are joined to the ascended Lord to share His health from heaven (Rom. 7:4; 8:11; 1 Cor. 6:13–15; 12:27).

11. Angels, assigned to serve a Christian who has been granted the gifts of healings, appear with the facial features and skin color of the nationality of that Christian. Believers are "from every tribe and tongue and people and nation" (Rev. 5:9), for God is not partial to any one nationality (Rom. 2:11).

12. In the last days a mighty outpouring of the Holy Spirit on all mankind is prophesied (Joel 2:28–29). This will be what the Bible calls the

"latter rain" (Joel 2:23), which comes in the spring to water again the fall planting. In Joel 2:30, God says that He will display wonders on the earth at that time.

"For you who fear My name the sun of righteousness will rise with healing in its wings" (Mal. 4:2). In these last days, believers will do greater works of healing than those Jesus did when He was first on the earth (John 14:12). If in the "early rain" following Pentecost, "they were all being healed" (Acts 5:16), how much more will the latter rain bring healings.

13. Two angels were present when Jesus rose from the dead (John 20:12). Resurrection is the ultimate healing. Angels are able to strengthen and encourage believers in their weakness (Dan. 10:10–11, 15–16, 19), to stand against the enemy (Dan. 10:12–13, 20), to help protect the believers (Dan. 6:22), and to relay instructions from God (Dan. 12:4).

    God gives general grace to the church as His healing agent through prayers, promising that "those who have believed... will lay hands on the sick, and they will recover" (Mark 16:17–18; James 5:14–15). Jesus sent the twelve out "to heal diseases" (Luke 9:1), and then later He sent the seventy out two by two to "heal those in [the city] who are sick" (Luke 10:9). The use of two believers to pray for the sick is in accordance with His Word: "If two of you agree on earth about anything that they may ask, it shall be done for them by My Father who is in heaven" (Matt. 18:19).

    But not all Christians are given the special grace that accompanies "the gifts of healings" (1 Cor. 12:30). This anointing to heal varies among believers. God empowers some believers with these manifestations to be used in the healing of particular kinds of infirmity or illness. The anointing may operate in one or more of the categories of healings such as: physical disease or debility, healing of emotions and the mind, deliverance from curses and the control of evil spirits, and healing of the wounded human spirit.

14. Jesus spoke the phrase "only believe" to the synagogue official when others reported to him that his young daughter had died (Luke 8:49–50). The Lord needed the father to trust Him, and He needed the faith of the three disciples He allowed to enter the room with Him where the child lay.

    Each believer needs the revelation of God's will for healing and health for His children, and he needs to receive the measure of Christ's faith allotted to each believer through the Scriptures (Rom. 12:3; Eph. 4:7).

15. The redeemed go immediately to heaven when their bodies die on earth (2 Cor. 5:8; Phil. 1:23). There their spirits are clothed with bodies of light similar to those of the angels. Each of the redeemed is recognizable in this spiritual body (Rev. 14:1, 4).

     Peter, James, and John on the mount of transfiguration could see, recognize, and hear Moses and Elijah (Luke 9:30, 33). The redeemed in heaven sing and praise God, serving Him (Rev. 14:1, 3; 7:9–10, 15). They await the day when they will receive glorified, resurrected bodies like the present body of the Lord Jesus (Luke 24:39; 1 John 3:2), so that they will be prepared to reign with Him on this present earth for a thousand years (Rev. 20:6).

16. "By His scourging [wounds or stripes] we are healed" (Isa. 53:5; 1 Pet. 2:24). The "we" in this passage includes human and angelic beings. Jesus had to be wounded in order for His atoning blood to be shed (Lev. 17:11; Heb. 9:22).

     The sin of the rebellious angels led by Lucifer affected the loyal host remaining in heaven. These good angels needed healing from the deep sorrow over the defection of many of their angelic friends. The peace of heaven was disturbed, and so the Father reconciled heaven also to Himself through His Son, "having made peace through the blood of His cross" (Col. 1:20).

     The Hebrew word for "stripes," *chabburah,* is pronounced "khab-boo-raw," the transliterated name of the angel who led the training meetings.

17. The anointing of a believer by the Holy Spirit with power to minister a spiritual gift or gifts is not constantly activated but is under the control of the Spirit. Jesus received the anointing of the Holy Spirit with power to minister when He returned from the forty days in the wilderness (Luke 4:14). He could exercise the anointing to heal the sick on certain occasions, as in Luke 5:17 and 6:19.

# Chapter 4
## Healing Angels

1. These body parts are not made of earthly flesh, blood, and bones, for nothing of the natural can be a part of heaven (1 Cor. 15:50). They are made of supernatural light (as are all created things in heaven), and they are the true body parts that God knows will be needed in the coming healing revival. The true and the good of everything on earth must originate in heaven (James 1:17; John 3:27; 1 Cor. 4:7; Heb. 9:23; 8:5). The God who knows the number of hairs of each head (Matt. 10:30) certainly knows each part of our bodies that will need replacement.

2. The last healing revival that occurred in America was in the 1950s, when God granted the "gifts of healings" to only a small number of Christians (1 Cor. 12:30).

3. The first promise made by God to the Israelites on their journey from bondage in Egypt concerned healing. He spoke it three days after they crossed the Red Sea (Exod. 15:22). He said that if they would heed His voice, do what is right in His sight, and obey His laws, then He would "put none of the diseases on you which I have put on the Egyptians; for I, the LORD, am your healer" (Exod. 15:26).

   Through the forty years of their wandering in the wilderness, God was faithful to His word and preserved them from sickness on a diet of bread from heaven and water (Deut. 8:4; Ps. 78:23–25; 105:41; 1 Cor. 10:4).

   God extended the promise of healing in body, soul, and spirit to all mankind who would repent of their sins and receive Christ as the new life within them (1 Thess. 5:23; Mark 16:17–18). This health is made possible by faith in His work on the cross of Calvary and in His resurrection and ascension into heaven (Isa. 53:4–5; Matt. 8:16–17). Matthew uses the same words, "healing every kind of disease and every kind of sickness," twice about Jesus and once about His disciples (Matt. 4:23; 9:35; 10:1). At one point in the life of the church in Jerusalem, all the sick and the demonized were being healed (Acts 5:16).

4. Christians through whom the Lord Jesus would exercise His healing ministry in a pure way must hate their natural self life (John 12:25; Luke 14:26) and the things of Satan's kingdom on the earth: "the lust

of the flesh and the lust of the eyes and the boastful pride of life" (1 John 2:15–17; James 4:3–4).

5. Demons are evil spirits who are part of Satan's forces. Those who work on the earth try to possess or oppress human beings who allow themselves to become vulnerable to their attack because of sin, deception, or ignorance (Deut. 32:16–17; 1 Tim. 4:1; 2 Cor. 2:11).

   There is much greater demonic activity recorded in the Gospels and the Book of Acts because of the ministry of Jesus Christ while on earth and of His disciples in the New Testament church. The Lord cast them out of afflicted people who came to Him, and so did His disciples (Matt. 8:16; Luke 10:17). Known as exorcism, or deliverance, or the casting out of evil spirits, this ministry has always had some part in the work of the church throughout the centuries.

6. The Hebrew word for "scourging" or "stripe," found in the phrase "by His scourging we are healed" (Isa. 53:5), is *chabburah,* the name of the instructor for these training sessions.

7. God the Holy Spirit imparts and sustains all life, whether it be in heaven or on earth (Acts 17:25; Job 12:10; 1 Tim. 6:13). The angelic beings are spirits (Heb. 1:14) whom God created by two means: (a) "by the word of the LORD" they were made, and (b) "by the breath of His mouth" they began to live (Ps. 33:6). God's breath, the Holy Spirit (Job 33:4), continually sustains the angels in life, and He is able to pass through them purely and powerfully to enliven other angels.

8. Through Christ Jesus, faith in God, as imparted through the Scriptures, is the basis of mankind's relationship with Him (Rom. 10:17; Heb. 11:6). When Jesus visited His hometown of Nazareth, "He could do no miracle there except that He laid His hands upon a few sick folk and healed them. And He wondered at their unbelief," or lack of faith (Mark 6:5–6). The people of Nazareth lost their faith in Jesus because "they took offense at Him" (Mark 6:3).

   Another time Jesus told the father of a child with severe epilepsy who was brought to Him for healing, "All things are possible to him who believes." The father replied that he believed but that he needed help with his unbelief (Mark 9:23–24). There was a mixture of faith and lack of faith in his heart, as there is with many Christians regarding healing through prayer (Matt. 7:11; James 1:6–8; 5:15).

9. When God covenanted with the Israelites at Mount Sinai (Horeb) to bless and multiply them if they would obey His laws, one of the

covenant promises rehearsed by Moses was to "remove from you all sickness…and not put on you any of the harmful diseases of Egypt which you have known" (Deut. 5:2; 7:15).

God made another covenant of blessings and curses with the Israelites in the land of Moab just before they crossed the Jordan into Canaan, again contingent upon their obedience (Deut. 28:1–2, 15). In verses 21–22, 27–28, 35, 58–61, and 65–66, God promised to bring upon them every sickness and plague known to man if they did not obey His commandments.

Under the New Covenant of grace through the shed blood of Christ Jesus, God promised that the Holy Spirit would put His laws in the hearts and minds of believers (Heb. 8:10). Their obedience would then originate from within them (even as sin does—Matt. 15:19). The Spirit plants the word of Christ in their hearts and then works to enable them to choose and do the will of God through Christ in them (Phil. 2:12–13; Rom. 6:17; 1 Cor. 12:6; Heb. 13:21). Christians "serve in newness of the [promptings of the] Spirit and not in oldness of the letter [of written rules]" (Rom. 7:6). How much more certain is the promise of healing by grace through faith in Christ (Mark 9:23) than that originally made to the Israelites under a covenant of law through their works (Heb. 8:6–9; Gal. 2:20–21; 3:5).

10. Believers abide in the New Covenant of grace through the shed blood of Christ by cooperating with the Holy Spirit in exercising that freedom of their will to choose Christ Jesus as the Lord: in every outer circumstance, in every thought and intention of their heart, and within their whole being. Therefore the members of the body are continually presented to God; the Lord Jesus is honored in their use (Col. 3:5; Rom. 6:12–13; 12:1), the power of the flesh to control the believer having been broken on the cross (Rom. 6:6–7).

Also, the old self is denied and laid aside as worthless (Matt. 16:24; Eph. 4:22; Col. 3:9). Its thoughts are taken captive to obey and to be set upon Christ (2 Cor. 10:5; Col. 3:2), and the whole mind is renewed by the new human spirit imparting the kind of thoughts He has (Eph. 4:23; Rom. 12:2). The natural emotions are not allowed to control the believer (Col. 3:5, 8; Eph. 4:31). By the Spirit he longs for God (Ps. 42:1–2) and the heart feelings of Christ (Eph. 4:23; Col. 3:12–13). The will is continually kept alert and active in siding with God's will and refusing the will of the enemy (Phil. 2:13; Rom. 12:2).

The new spiritual self (Eph. 4:24; Col. 3:10) of heart and human spirit (1 Pet. 3:4) seeks to know and do the will of God by being guided through the peace of Christ acting as umpire and guardian (Phil. 4:7; Col. 3:15); the conscience witnessing as to whether Christ's life is flowing or death (Gen. 2:9, 16–17; Deut. 30:19); and the enlightening of the Word concerning Christ, as quickened by the Holy Spirit, as to whether the faith of Jesus is being exercised or not (Heb. 4:12; Rom. 10:17; 14:23).

11. The name of one of the healing angels is Rapha, the Hebrew word meaning "to heal." The other healing angel is Raphashanah, the addition being the Hebrew word *shanah* meaning "to repeat or do again." They looked like a matching pair.

12. Angels have bodies of light that can be seen and felt. We know this because an angel touched Elijah twice, and the touch awakened him from sleep (1 Kings 19:5, 7). Jacob wrestled all night with an angel and held on to him (Gen. 32:24–26). An angel touched Daniel as he lay on the ground prostrate and set the prophet on his hands and knees (Dan. 10:10, 18).

# Chapter 5
## The Lord Jesus

1. Jesus is the greater Joseph and wears "the true" of Joseph's varicolored cloak (Gen. 37:3; Heb. 8:2). The Hebrew word for such a garment is *pas,* which means that it was a full-length tunic, reaching to the hands and the feet. The ordinary tunic reached only to the knees and was usually without sleeves. The multicoloring of Jesus' garment signifies the multifaceted aspects of His glorious ministry.

2. The resurrected body of the Lord Jesus was able to pass through a closed door on earth (John 20:19, 26). He is "Lord of all" (Acts 10:36), all things having been put in subjection to Him (Eph. 1:22). It is not strange that His resurrection body can assume a form (Mark 16:12) that can enter a human being on earth who is also "light in the Lord" (Eph. 5:8).

3. Ezekiel saw four cherubim (Ezek. 10:20), each of these heavenly creatures having four faces (Ezek. 1:5–10; 10:20): the face of a man in front, the face of a lion on the right side, the face of a bull on the left side, and the face of an eagle behind. One interpretation of these faces is that they represent the four aspects of the ministry of Christ Jesus: man as priest, lion as king, bull as servant, and eagle as prophet. The Lord Jesus, facing out in the position of the eagle, was a tactile sign that one could feel, as with Ezekiel eating the scroll of God's Word (Ezek. 3:1–3).

4. Here is another tactile sign of the Lord opening human eyes to see spiritual realities, in the same way that He offered eye salve to the Laodiceans (Rev. 3:18).

5. When the Lord puts His cloak over someone but does not require the other's cloak, it signifies His initiating a unilateral or one–sided covenant. Jesus pledges His love and loyalty, as did Jonathan to David in total commitment by his giving the Lord's anointed his cloak, his armor, and all of his weapons (1 Sam. 18:3–4).

6. To put your hand over your mouth signifies consternation and the inability to speak further. Job did this when God spoke with him (Job 40:4).

7. If humans are able to walk on water when the Lord bids them to do so, then they are able to fly when the Lord wills it (Matt. 14:28–29).

8. To call the Lord Jesus to the mountains of spices is to urge Him to manifest the sweet aroma of His perfection through the believer without delay (Song of Sol. 8:14; 2 Cor. 2:14–15).

Here follows a description of the spices:

## Myrrh: Obedience Unto Death

The spice myrrh comes from a thick gum that flows from the pierced bark of a knotted, thorny tree. The gum hardens into red drops called "tears." The word *myrrh* comes from a primary root in Hebrew meaning "bitter suffering." The Greek word denotes a spice used in burial. In the New Testament, the Magi brought gifts to the Christ child, including myrrh, a foreshadowing of His suffering and bitter death on the cross (Matt. 2:11).

The original sense of the word is that of "distilling in drops"—a slow process of purification. Christ lived a life of distillation, for "although He was a Son, He learned obedience from the things which He suffered" (Heb. 5:8). Jesus emptied Himself of His own will, and this culminated in obedience to the point of death on a cross (Phil. 2:7–8). Likewise, each child of God is called to smell of the myrrh of distillation day after day, by denying his or her own self life and walking in obedience to the will of Christ alone (Matt. 16:24–25; 6:10).

## Cinnamon: Holiness of Heart

The primary root of the word *cinnamon* means "emitting an odor." The spice is harvested in quills of the fragrant, inner bark of a tree of the laurel family.

In the Song of Solomon, cinnamon grows in the locked garden that Jesus says is "my sister, my bride" (Song of Sol. 4:12–14). The new heart of each believer is a garden with fragrant spices—a heart enclosed and set apart for the Lord Jesus alone—as the heart of Jesus is undivided in His consecration unto the Father alone (2 Chron. 16:9; Luke 10:22).

In Proverbs 7:10, the adulterous woman, "dressed as a harlot and cunning of heart," has sprinkled her bed with fragrant spices that also include cinnamon (Prov. 7:17), a counterfeit of the heart of the bride. She flings her heart open to embrace every sort of spiritual adultery.

In both instances, cinnamon emits an odor: either of consecration in holiness unto the Lord (Exod. 30:23–25, 30; Lev. 8:12), which is sweet in the nostrils of God, or the corrupted odor of deception and seduction (Prov. 7:17–19), which is a stench to Him.

## Cassia: Homage to God Alone

Cassia is also from the laurel family, smelling and tasting somewhat like cinnamon but considered inferior to it, a humbler plant. God exalts this lowly tree to provide one of the four spices used in the holy anointing oil (Exod. 30:23–25). Its name, representative of its properties, comes from a root word meaning "to bow down," "to stoop," "to pay homage," depicting the humility of Christ before His Father. Jesus said, "I honor My Father...I do not seek My glory" (John 8:49–50). Although as believers we are to show ourselves humble before others (1 Pet. 2:17; 5:5), we are to bow down in worship to God alone (2 Kings 17:35–36; Matt. 4:10).

The word *homage* means "to show a reverential fidelity and respect" (Exod. 34:8). We, like Jesus, are to reverence our Father with holy fear and veneration, treating Him as sacred in the sight of others (Num. 20:10–12; Ezek. 36:22–23) and in the depths of our hearts (1 Pet. 3:15).

## Calamus: Uprightness

Calamus is a fragrant oil derived from a marsh plant known as sweet flag. The Hebrew word for this spice means "a stalk or a reed (as erect)," or upright. We see a biblical meaning of upright in the first instance of that Hebrew word in Scripture, being translated "right in [God's] sight" (Exod. 15:26). God's poetic name for His people Israel was "Jeshurun," a word meaning "upright one" (Isa. 44:2). In His Father's eyes the Lord Jesus was upright in Himself (Ps. 25:8), in His words (Ps. 33:4), and in His ways (Isa. 11:4).

The second biblical meaning of upright includes also that of being smooth and straight, that is, without deviation, a true and direct course. Everything about Jesus Christ is in true alignment with who the Father is. There is no obstruction or unevenness in Him to hinder the clear revelation of God (John 5:30; 14:9). Christians, like John the Baptist, are to "make straight the way of the Lord" (John 1:23), so that God's Son may be seen and heard through them without any obstacle of their "flesh" (Rom. 7:25; Gal. 6:8). Isaiah cried, "O Upright One, make the path of the righteous level" (Isa. 26:7), so that their walk is straight toward God.

## Henna: Forgiveness

Henna, translated "camphire" in the King James Version, comes from a tree whose leaves yield a stain used as a red dye. The Hebrew word means "to cover, a redemption price." The primary root of the word means "to forgive." Therefore this fragrant spice signifies the shed blood of Christ on Calvary as our ransom from sin and death (1 Tim. 2:6).

In the Middle East on the night before a wedding, the bride has henna paste bound to the palms of her hands and soles of her feet. In Christian symbolism her hands (works) and feet (walk) are to exude the sweet smell of forgiveness and show forth the red stain of His shed blood on the cross. Christ calls His bride to walk continually cleansed through the forgiveness won for her by her Bridegroom (1 John 1:9) and to pass that forgiveness on to others (Matt. 6:14–15).

## Aloes: Intimacy

The word *aloes* is from an Arabic word meaning "little tents," descriptive of the three-cornered shape of the capsules of the lignaloes tree whose resin is fragrant.

The small, pointed tent is the type spoken of in 2 Samuel 16:22, meaning a "pleasure tent on the housetop" or a "bridal tent": a place of intimacy. Outside the camp Moses pitched a private tent of meeting where God spoke to him face to face (Exod. 33:7, 9, 11). David also erected such a tent on Mount Zion for the ark of the covenant, where he could be as close as possible to the presence of the Lord (2 Sam. 6:17). Jesus has perfect intimacy with His Father, an intimacy into which we are being perfected: "As Thou, Father, art in Me, and I in Thou, that they also may be in Us" (John 17:21, 23). Our constant heart's cry should be to go with Him into the intimacy of the bridal tent that He might know us and we Him (John 10:14–15). Only through intimacy in spirit with Jesus do we bring forth spiritual children for His kingdom (1 John 1:3; Gal. 4:19; 1 Cor. 4:15).

## Nard: Light

Pure nard is a very costly spice. It is produced from the hairy, dried stems of a plant grown at heights up to thirteen thousand feet in the Himalayas in the purer, stronger light of the sun. The word *nard* (spikenard in the King James Version) is from the Hebrew root meaning "light."

God's reality in heaven is visible by the pure, uncreated light of

His nature. He is light, and there is no darkness in Him (1 John 1:5). His Son, Christ Jesus, is the true light from the Father (John 1:9)— the reality of God made visible in a human being (John 1:14). There is no darkness of sin in Him, for He walks in the light of His Father (John 8:29; 1 John 1:7).

Christians are to live their lives before God and man truthfully, being the same person outwardly as they are within their hearts. We are to be the transparent lamps through which the heavenly light of Christ shines (Rom. 13:12). As bearers of His light, we are to cooperate with the Holy Spirit as He takes His stand against all darkness within us (Eph. 5:8). Eventually even our shadows are to be so infused with the light of God that as we pass, the sick are healed (Acts 5:15).

## *Saffron: Faith*

Saffron is a very expensive spice. It is collected from the three tiny, orange-red stigmas of the flowers of the crocus sativus. About two hundred twenty-five thousand of these stigmas must be picked out by hand to produce one pound of saffron. This extremely valuable spice is yellow-gold in color when dried, and it is literally worth its weight in gold. Medicinally it strengthens the heart. For these reasons, saffron is symbolic of the faith Jesus Christ held in His heart toward His heavenly Father (Heb. 2:13). His faith in His Father's words to Him was tested and perfected (Heb. 12:2) throughout His ministry years on earth, beginning with the first temptation in the wilderness (Matt. 4:3–4).

By grace through faith we are saved (Eph. 2:8). By faith we live (Hab. 2:4), and it is perfected faith that Christ is seeking when He returns. "However, when the Son of man comes, will He find (persistence in) the faith on the earth?" (Luke 18:8, AMP). Therefore we rejoice in trials so "that the proof of [our] faith, being more precious than gold which is perishable, even though tested by fire, may be found to result in praise and glory and honor at the revelation of Jesus Christ" (1 Pet. 1:7).

## *Frankincense: Purity*

Frankincense is a gum resin that flows from the inner wood of a tree resembling the mountain ash. The word in Hebrew comes from a root meaning "pure" or "white" because of the glittering, milk-white, resin "tears." These tears, when burned, give off a strong, balsam odor. The finest incense contains pure frankincense, rising in white smoke to symbolize the prayers that ascend to the throne of God (Rev. 8:3–4). Frankincense represents the purity of the consecration of the resurrected Christ in His ministry on our behalf before the Father (Rom. 8:34). Our Lord Jesus has sanctified or set Himself apart (John 17:19) unto the Father as the "holy, innocent, undefiled" high priest (Heb. 7:25–26), in order to "redeem us from every lawless deed and to purify for Himself a people for His own possession" (Titus 2:14).

When Christ appears in glory, "we shall be like Him, because we shall see Him just as He is. And everyone who has this hope fixed on Him purifies himself, just as He is pure" (1 John 3:2–3).

## Onycha: Authority

The Hebrew word for the rockrose, *onycha,* comes from the root meaning "to roar" or "a lion." The resurrected Lord is the Lion of the tribe of Judah, who has been given all authority in heaven and on earth (Rev. 5:5; Matt. 28:18), with power "to subject all things to Himself" (Phil. 3:21). The Father's authority through Christ is symbolized in the roar of the lion in Hosea 11:10–11: "They will follow behind Yahweh; He will be roaring like a lion—how he will roar!...and his sons will come speeding from Egypt like a bird, speeding from the land of Assyria like a dove" (JB).

The smell emitted by onycha in the holy incense not only testifies to Christ's authority, His lordship here on earth, but as it rises through the mid-heaven, daily it reminds Satan that he is a defeated foe. Christians share in Christ's authority "to tread upon...all the power of the enemy" in His name (Luke 10:19).

## Galbanum:
## Worship, Praise, Adoration, and Thanksgiving

The Hebrew for the word *galbanum* is from a primary root meaning "fat" or "the richest or choicest part" or "the best." The spice is a gum resin collected by slicing the stems of the plants of the ferula family. Fat was one of the two parts of the animal sacrifice that was entirely reserved for God (Lev. 3:16–17). It signified the finest offering that could be given to Him, that which was beyond all else in pleasing Him: joyful worship "in spirit and truth" (Deut. 28:47; John 4:23).

Satan promised "the kingdoms of the world and their glory" to Christ in exchange for His worship (Matt. 4:8–9). The enemy drives unbelievers to seek "the fat" of this age—to receive praise, worship, gratitude, and adoration for themselves (John 5:44). In direct opposition to the Word of God (Isa. 42:8), many in the body of Christ are spiritually overweight from taking to themselves that which belongs to God alone: the fat.

# *Stacte: Truth With Mercy*

Stacte is from the root meaning "to fall in drops" or "to prophesy." Since "the testimony of Jesus is the spirit of prophecy" (Rev. 19:10), the holy incense (of which this spice is a part [Exod. 30:34–35]) prophesied of Christ to God, but it also struck terror into those who were enemies of Christ (Josh. 2:9–11). The aroma of the incense rising from the tabernacle ascended to the throne in heaven and went throughout the camp. It also could be smelled for miles, even across the Jordan by the Canaanites (2 Cor. 2:15–16). It testified to the truth of salvation in Christ alone (John 14:6), for our Father wishes all men to be saved (1 Tim. 2:3–4). The truth of Christ, of which stacte prophesied, "fell in drops" or softly, mercifully. Proverbs 16:6 says, "By mercy and truth iniquity is purged: and by the fear of the LORD men depart from evil" (KJV). Rahab the harlot must have been among those who smelled this prophetic testimony of Jesus—the Way, the Truth, and the Life—and who feared God and believed into the salvation He provided (Josh. 2:11–13).

9. A dove with an olive leaf in its beak is a symbol of peace. That bird returned to Noah in the ark with this evidence that the waters of judgment had subsided and that God was at peace with the earth (Gen. 8:8–11).

   God gave the levitical priest Phinehas and his descendants "My covenant of peace...because he was jealous for his God and made atonement for the sins of Israel," turning away God's wrath from destroying them (Num. 25:11–13; Mal. 2:4–6).

   The Levites camped directly around the tabernacle on all four sides so that, by their position between God and the people, God's wrath for the sins of the Israelites might be averted (Num. 1:53).

   Jesus "made peace [with the Father] through the blood of His cross" (Col. 1:20; Rom. 5:1). Under the New Covenant, the holy priesthood of God's people may intercede through Christ our High Priest (Heb. 7:25–26; 1 Pet. 2:5) on behalf of other believers who commit sin; God will, for the intercessor, grant life to the sinner (1 John 5:16).

10. The fire of God, the Holy Spirit, is coming to the church to touch all those who call themselves Christians. God's fire will burn away all that is not of Christ (Matt. 3:12; 1 Cor. 3:11–13). It is able to set ablaze the sacrificial offering of the new heart with flaming passion for the Lord Jesus (Song of Sol. 8:6; 1 Kings 18:38). We are to learn to love "the spirit of burning" that brings His glory as a canopy over all (Isa. 4:3–5).

11. God created the first human beings to live in a garden with Him (Gen. 2:8; 3:8). His re-creation of the human race also began in a garden where He rose from the dead (John 19:41; Matt. 28:1, 6). Every garden that God plants is to honor His Son: first, the Garden of Eden in heaven (Ezek. 28:13); then the copy of that heavenly garden that was on earth (Heb. 9:23–24); and finally the individual, private garden in the new heart of every believer (Song of Sol. 4:12–16). In order to tend this interior garden, we are to keep it clean and pure from adulteration by the world, the flesh, and the devil.

    Every believer who is in love with Christ is that garden in the new heart (Song of Sol. 4:12), to be kept locked and sealed for Jesus alone to meet us there. It is a garden with a selection of the delicious fruit of His character (Gal. 5:22–23) and an assortment of spice plants and trees to waft the fragrance of His perfections of virtue abroad (2 Cor. 2:14–15); His beauty is represented by a unique planting of flowers (Song of Sol. 6:2–3). The Father selects those aspects of His Son that He delights to have grown and manifested in each, new heart (1 Cor. 12:4–7, 11; Rom. 12:3, 6; Eph. 4:7). This is true, eternal individuality, and it comes from God.

12. "Until the cool of the day when the shadows flee away, turn, my beloved, and be like a gazelle or a young stag on the mountains of Bether" (Song of Sol. 2:17).

13. Jesus said in Scripture that His burden or load was light because the yoke of responsibility He carried was easy (Matt. 11:30). This was true because He did nothing on His own initiative (John 5:30). The Father gave Him all those who were to be saved and resurrected (John 6:38–40). Furthermore, He lost none of those given Him by the Father. He relied not on His own strength but by accomplishing all in the power of the Holy Spirit (John 16:14). The Lord promised those who walk in step with Him and share His burden would find rest (Matt. 11:29) instead of the heavy load of trying to obey legalistic rules and rituals by their own efforts (Luke 11:46).

14. In eternity all things are complete and present to God, but in time they are not complete (Rev. 21:5–6). The Lord Jesus longs for the completion of the full number of the redeemed, adopted children to stand before the Father and before the Lamb (Rev. 7:9): "a kingdom, priests to His God and Father" (Rev. 1:6), "bond-servants [who] shall serve Him" and "shall see His face" (Rev. 22:3–4).

15. At the end, the Lord Jesus will "[deliver] up the kingdom to the God and Father" after "He has put all His enemies under His feet" so that

the Father "may be all in all" (1 Cor. 15:24–25, 28). The Son will have raised up to eternal life all that the Father had given to Him, all those who have believed in Christ (John 6:39–40).

16. God is love (1 John 4:7–8). His children know love by the Father giving Himself to them through His Son (1 John 4:9). The Father's love is incarnate in His Son, and the Holy Spirit makes that love flow in us (John 15:9; 17:26; Rom. 5:5) as we love the brethren (John 15:12; 1 John 4:11–12).

17. The tears of godly sorrow that lead to repentance in those who are in sin and the tears of those who intercede for them are very precious to God. They are preserved in His bottle and recorded in His book of remembrance (2 Cor. 7:9–10; Phil. 3:18; Ps. 56:8; Mal. 3:16).

    The tears of God, like those of a woman in the labor of childbirth (Gal. 4:19; Rev. 12:2), are shed as He births His children (Isa. 42:14). He also moans and weeps about the extermination He must carry out upon a nation like Moab because of its sins (Jer. 48:31–32). Jesus was a man of sorrows with regret in His heart over the loss those would suffer who reject Him (Luke 23:28–30).

18. In Scripture one's name may signify one's character, position, function, or destiny before God, the name being practically equivalent to the person. Jesus, along with every Jewish baby boy, was named at His circumcision to signify His entrance into the covenant (Gen. 17:10–12; Luke 2:21). To each believer who overcomes with Christ, a new and everlasting name will be given by the Lord. The saint will be called by this new name in heaven, and he will be forever in covenant with Him, the new name being permanently inscribed on a white stone (Rev. 2:17). The stone is a witness to the sealing in covenant, as the stone was when Joshua made a covenant with the Israelites at Shechem (Josh. 24:25–27).

    The Lord builds His church with living stones (1 Pet. 2:5), those who receive the revelation of Him as the Christ. Simon did, and his name was changed to *Peter,* meaning "a stone" (Matt. 16:16–18). The Lord will reign in His thousand-year kingdom on earth with those white, living stones who through Him have overcome all of their enemies (Rev. 20:4–6) and have learned to live hidden in God (Col. 3:3–4).

19. The Lord must call each person to Himself before the new birth can occur (Acts 2:39; 2 Thess. 2:14). Jesus said that "the [spiritually] dead shall hear the voice of the Son of God; and those who hear shall live" (John 5:25; Rom. 8:30). The words of Christ summoning a

person to Himself "are spirit and are life," imparting the Holy Spirit to those who will receive them (John 6:63). He may begin calling a person while he or she is still in the womb (Isa. 49:1). The Lord Jesus experiences the pain of deep longing as He waits for those whom He created for Himself to stop trifling with the gods of this world (Isa. 65:1–2; Phil. 1:8).

20. As we enter the End Times, many in the church "will fall away and will [betray] one another and hate one another" to save themselves from suffering (Matt. 24:10). "You will be [betrayed] even by parents and brothers and relatives and friends, and they will put some of you to death, and you will be hated by all on account of My name" (Luke 21:16–17). Three stages of betrayal of the Lord, as portrayed by Judas, are: 1) those who pretend to be His disciples but secretly love the things of the world (John 12:6); 2) those who secretly consort with His enemies (Matt. 26:14–16); and 3) those who openly side with His enemies (Matt. 26:47–49).

# Chapter 6
## The Eagle's Nest

1. The "river of the water of life" in heaven is a visible representation of the Holy Spirit providing life to everything there (Rev. 22:1). Even on earth God grants to His faithful children "to drink of the river of Thy delights. For with Thou is the fountain of life" (Ps. 36:8–9). The Hebrew word for *river* means "a wadi or the channel of a watercourse that is dry except when it rains" (a symbol of the Spirit outpoured—Hos. 6:3), and then it becomes an overflowing river. This spiritual river is the powerful moving of the Holy Spirit supplying eternal life to and through those who obey Him (John 4:14; 7:38–39; Acts 5:32).

   We are entering "the last days" (2 Tim. 3:1; 2 Pet. 3:3) when the Holy Spirit will be outpoured in a mightier way than ever before (Joel 2:28–29) as the promised "latter rain" that will bring in a worldwide harvest (Joel 2:23–24). The Spirit will then move through the earth—as the river described in Ezekiel 47:1, 5, and 9—to bring life wherever He flows.

2. The streams that come out from the inspiration of the river of the Holy Spirit are the various movements (such as denominations) of the people of God in Christ who together form His living church on earth. These streams are not independent, for they not only drink from the one Spirit (1 Cor. 12:13–14), but they also add their particular contribution back into the flow of the Spirit in the one church (1 Cor. 12:7; Eph. 4:4, 16).

   The coming descent of the Holy Spirit will be in such fullness of power that it will be necessary for these streams of God's people to be bound together in "one heart and soul" (Acts 4:32). This unity in the Holy Spirit (Eph. 4:3; 1 Cor. 12:25–26) will be needed to utilize in purity all the gifts and graces from the Spirit so as to preserve His work from corruption or waste.

3. The sword of the Spirit is the living Word of God concerning Christ Jesus as applied by the Holy Spirit (Eph. 6:17; Heb. 4:12; Rev. 19:13–15). In the coming days we pray that the Lord Jesus will send forth His Word to the various churches as He did in the second and third chapters of Revelation. He depends upon those who overcome by walking above their flesh, the world, and the devil: saints who no longer live for anything but for Him (2 Cor. 5:14–15; Phil. 1:20–21; 2:21).

The ribbons in the vision represent those streams or bodies of believers who are pliable and willing to be rolled up by the Spirit to wait for His use (Hab. 2:3; Mic. 7:7). The spindles are long rods on which the spools may easily rotate as the ribbons are unwound and sewn together.

4. The heavenly city of God is "the Jerusalem above [which] is free; she is our mother" (Gal. 4:26; Heb. 11:16; 12:22). The earthly copy of that city is the church of the living God described in Psalm 46:4–5: "There is a river [the Spirit flowing freely] whose streams make glad the city of God, the holy dwelling places of the Most High. God is in the midst of her, she will not be moved."

5. Oil is a type of the anointing with power that the Holy Spirit bestows upon believers so that Christ Jesus from heaven will be able to minister through them for the bringing in of His kingdom here on earth (Exod. 30:25, 30; Acts 1:8; 2:33; 1 Cor. 4:20). There is a vast supply of this oil that God has reserved for a fuller "salvation ready to be revealed in the last time" (1 Pet. 1:5; Rom. 8:18–19). It will come as a gusher, which is an oil well that spouts forth of itself without being pumped by man. The members of that unified, true church will dwell together as brethren, all of them having a share in the anointing oil that comes down from Jesus, who is their head (Ps. 133; 1 John 3:14). "Spindle Top" was one of the greatest oil gushers in recorded history.

6. The Lord quotes Revelation 19:10. The white Eagle is the risen Lord Jesus in His pure and righteous ministry as the prophet of God, for everything about Him is white (Matt. 17:2; Rev. 1:14; 3:4). A prophet, like the eagle, discerns clearly the things on earth from the height of God's viewpoint; he speaks words from God (Deut. 18:18; John 7:16–18; 12:49–50). The Lord carried the children of Israel safely through their wilderness wanderings as "on eagles' wings" (Exod. 19:4), a figure of speech signifying His supernatural deliverance that, like the eagle's flight, the world cannot provide (Deut. 8:15–16).

7. An eagle's nest is used for many years; through the years the eagle may enlarge the nest up to six feet high and five feet wide. The white Eagle, the Lord Jesus, shares His nest, which is on a rocky ledge on a mountain height, with those who are learning to fly with Him in spirit. Spiritually, His nest represents a place of rest, quietness, and intimacy with Him (Ps. 31:20; 63:7; 91:1–2, 4, 9, 14). This is a place where one learns to trust Him as God's everything, and so as one's everything (Col. 3:11; John 3:35).

# Notes

8. The paper doll Christians copy one another by using standardized methods of ministry employed in the church, or they attempt to reproduce the kind of ministry that was effective in the life of a famous minister of the past. They may try to duplicate the conditions that brought revival at another location. This use of patterns and formulas is actually a form of divination (a method of obtaining results in the spiritual realm without God's help), which He will not tolerate. Satan will often supply some of his limited power to this occult practice to advance his evil purposes. The false prophets in the Old Testament would repeat each other's words or pronounce prophecies that God had not given them (Jer. 14:14; 23:30; Ezek. 22:28).

   The Pharisees obeyed complicated rules and rituals of behavior, but their reverence for God consisted of tradition learned by rote (Isa. 29:13). The Lord refused to copy both the customs of the Pharisees and the God-inspired fasting of John the Baptist (Luke 5:33). He listened and watched for His Father's instructions moment by moment (John 5:19–20, 30).

9. This kind of Christian is rare. This disciple "hates his [soul] life [mind, emotions, and will] in this world" so that he may have the soul life of Christ forever (John 12:25). He is not at home on earth (2 Cor. 5:8; Phil. 1:23), for he cannot be satisfied by anything in this present world system (1 John 2:15, 17; 5:19). He desires only to feed upon the Lord Jesus as the hand of the Father shares His Son with him by the Spirit (Hos. 11:4; Ps. 78:23–25; John 6:32–35, 57).

   Jesus' food is to please and honor His Father in everything (John 4:32, 34; 8:29). Jesus alone nourishes the Father (Lev. 21:6; Num. 28:2; Ezek. 44:7). As His Son is the true bread and drink (John 6:51, 55), Jesus alone sustains such a Christian. In time, this kind of believer will be perfected into oneness with the Son and the Father so that he is, acts, and looks like Jesus who is formed within him (John 17:21, 23; Gal. 4:19; 2 Cor. 4:10–12).

10. The lofty eagle flies alone or with his mate, soaring effortlessly on the thermal currents; he builds his nest as high as possible. He has binocular vision, a symbol of the believer whose spiritual eyes Christ, the great Eagle, has opened (Matt. 13:16–17; Eph. 1:18–19). This Christian is at home in the godly spiritual world (1 Cor. 2:9–10; Phil. 3:20). He "[seeks] the things above, where Christ is," setting his mind upon the things of God (Col. 3:1–2).

    The gift of the Holy Spirit enables the Spirit to bear witness of Christ in the saint (John 15:26), first to God the Father (Acts 2:3–4; 1 Cor. 14:2) and then to others (Acts 2:5, 9–11; 1:8).

11. Hesitation or delay in following the Lord indicates that the allotted measure of the Lord's faith is not being exercised in the spiritual heart of the believer (Rom. 12:3). Christ's love within that one has not become full (Eph. 3:19; Gal. 5:6). We see an example of this hesitation in the maiden whom Jesus is inviting to share more of His life (Song of Sol. 5:2–5). He asks her to open her heart to bear some of His sufferings. She delays by resorting to reasoning. She then agrees to His requst, but He has gone away. She must now endure pain of another kind: the loss of consciousness of God's presence, as Jesus experienced on the cross (Song of Sol. 5:6; Matt. 27:46).

# Chapter 7
## Obedience

1. Ezekiel 28:13 describes Lucifer in heaven before he betrayed God. The end of the verse may be translated "and the gold, the workmanship of your tambourines and flutes, was prepared in you on the day you were created." Apparently he was connected in some way with worship in heaven. These musical instruments were "in" him, no doubt as part of his attire.

2. Gold is a symbol of Christ Jesus or the manifestation of the glory of that which honors God (Song of Sol. 5:11; Job 23:10). It is the one metallic element described in the Garden of Eden, indicating the value and beauty of the earth He had brought into being (Gen. 2:11–12). All the sacred objects in the tent of the tabernacle were of pure gold, for only the most precious metal was to be used to represent God in His dwelling place among the Israelites (Exod. 25:17–18, 24, 31; 37:25–26). This is true on earth because it is true of the original tabernacle in heaven (Rev. 8:3).

3. Bound to the foreheads of the Israelites were little boxes, known as phylacteries, that contained verses of Scripture (Deut. 11:18). God instituted this custom in order to remind them that the truth of His words were to be impressed upon their minds and their hearts, so that they were on their lips wherever they were and whatever they were doing (Deut. 11:19). His Word says that all creation is to praise Him continually (Ps. 148:2; 34:1).

4. God assigns angels and other heavenly beings to serve on earth "those who will inherit salvation" (Heb. 1:14; Gen. 48:16; Exod. 23:23). Angels may be assigned to a human being for life (Matt. 18:10), or for a certain period of time (Acts 7:38), or for one visit (Luke 1:26). The service rendered by angels includes assistance to believers in developing spiritual gifts and callings (Judg. 6:12–16). Judy is a feminine form of the biblical name *Judah,* which means "praise." A life of praise is so important for those who follow the Lord that God assigns angels to help believers express it in blessing God and in binding His enemies (Ps. 34:1; 149:6–9).

5. Praise is to be offered to the Father through the Son by the Holy Spirit in believers. The Son's words of praise to His Father contain

something of the divine nature, heart, and life (John 6:63; Heb. 2:11–12). Therefore this true praise is substantial, active, alive, and visible in the spiritual realm (Heb. 4:12). Worship in the Spirit of God by the believers on earth is joined to the praise in heaven because their resurrected, human spirits here are one with the spirit of the Lord Jesus there (Phil. 3:3; 1 Cor. 6:17; Eph. 2:6).

6. Praise to God may come from the playing of a musical instrument (Ps. 150:3–5). It is possible "to prophesy with lyres, harps, and cymbals," that is, to speak messages from God with their sounds (1 Chron. 25:1).

7. The living church of Christ Jesus is being watched with great anticipation by the host of heaven, both the redeemed there and the angels (Heb. 12:1). Paul says that "the anxious longing of the creation [including angels] waits eagerly for the revealing of the sons of God" in the last times (Rom. 8:19; 1 Pet. 1:5–6). Jesus said that "there is joy in the presence of the angels of God over one sinner who repents" (Luke 15:10). How much more do they exult when the church worships (Rev. 7:9–11).

8. All God's children must learn to obey Him, even as Jesus on earth had to learn in His human nature to obey His Father in all things (Heb. 5:8; John 8:29). The natural person of believers is incapable of obeying God, for their "flesh" (the earthly body and soul acting on its own) desires only to do what it pleases (Rom. 8:7; 7:18; Eph. 2:3). Therefore our obedience must be learned by repeated acts of the will in freely choosing moment by moment the obedience of Jesus' perfect human nature in us (Eph. 4:24; Col. 3:10). The Holy Spirit can then reinforce the flow of the Lord's obedient life in us (Heb. 5:9; Phil. 2:13). Christ has been made unto us all things, including the obedience that the Father desires (1 Cor. 1:30; Col. 3:11). Believers need to let Christ manifest the life of obedience in them, for He is the only life in them (Isa. 26:12; 2 Cor. 4:10–11; John 14:13–14, 19; Col. 3:4).

9. The natural or earthly self is the greatest hindrance to following the Lord, therefore it must be set aside (Matt. 16:24). The earthly soul life must be replaced by the soul life of Jesus' perfect human nature in us (Matt. 16:25). This exchange is called the salvation of the soul (Luke 21:19; Heb. 10:39; James 1:21; 1 Pet. 1:9). The Holy Spirit cannot protect us when we allow the devil and his demons to work through our old self (Gen. 4:7; Eph. 4:27; 1 Pet. 5:8–9). We give legal permission to them to inhabit the darkness in us because of sin (Eph. 5:11).

# Notes

10. The glory of Christ's love meets all of the believer's true needs (John 17:24; Phil. 4:19). The enemy is capable of stimulating our natural desires so that we feel we must have certain earthly gratifications and have them now (1 Pet. 1:14). We can come to rely upon these substitutes and to love them instead of loving the Lord (1 John 2:15–16). We can discover that "the love of Christ [for us] controls us" (2 Cor. 5:14); that His love is better than wine (earth's best stimulants) (Song of Sol. 1:2); and that His "love never fails" us (1 Cor. 13:8). It is no sacrifice to choose that which is of God in Christ—eternal, divine, truly pleasurable, and satisfying—instead of that which is temporary, created, a counterfeit pleasure, and a false satisfaction (James 4:3–4; 1 John 2:17).

11. Every believer must "forsake...his thoughts" because "every intent of the thoughts of his heart [is] only evil continually...from his youth" (Isa. 55:7; Gen. 6:5; 8:21). The Holy Spirit transforms us by helping us set our renewed minds (no longer conformed to this world) on God's interests (Matt. 16:23; Eph. 4:23; Rom. 12:2).

12. The Lord Jesus said that the path that leads to true life is narrow and restricted to walking step by step in Him who is the way (Matt. 7:14; 1 John 1:7).

13. Paul tells us that the imaginations and speculations of the mind of the natural person are vain and futile because they focus upon "the creature rather than the Creator" (Rom. 1:21, 25).

14. God said that the root of sin in mankind is in the thoughts of our hearts (Gen. 6:5). Jesus reiterated that truth (Matt. 15:18–19). The enemy has erected his fortresses in our natural minds in the form of man-centered attitudes, speculations, and beliefs (2 Cor. 10:4–5). From these citadels his demons can deceive and torment the believer, as happened to the slave with the unforgiving attitude in Jesus' parable (Matt. 18:33–35).

15. Paul says that the unruly mind can be reclaimed for Christ by casting down speculations and every proud argument that is contrary to the true knowledge of God in Scripture. The believer then takes control of every thought to make it obedient to Christ (2 Cor. 10:5).

16. The young apostle Peter was headstrong, bent on going wherever he wished (John 21:3). Jesus told him that when he grew old, he would have to follow His Master in the way of the cross where he did not wish to go (John 21:18–19).

17. The name *Shama* is a Hebrew word meaning "to hear with the intent to be obedient." An example of this word is spoken by Moses to the children of Israel to "listen obediently to the voice of the LORD your God." (Deut. 15:5).

18. God's "eyes are too pure to approve evil, and [He] canst not look on wickedness with favor" (Hab. 1:13). "Your iniquities have made a separation between you and your God, and your sins have hidden His face [intimacy] from you" (Isa. 59:2). The light of God cannot fellowship with darkness (1 John 1:6).

19. "Delight yourself in the LORD; and He will give you the desires of your heart" (Ps. 37:4). "In Thy presence is fulness of joy; in Thy right hand there are pleasures forever" (Ps. 16:11). "Thou dost give them to drink of the river of Thy delights" (Ps. 36:8). "God has prepared for those who love Him" things never seen or heard before, things beyond imagination (1 Cor. 2:9).

20. Jesus in His human nature "learned obedience from the things which He suffered" (Heb. 5:8). Faith was perfected in Him as He endured the rejection and betrayal of those He came to save. Having "emptied Himself, taking the form of a bond-servant," He became "obedient to the point of death, even death on a cross" (Phil. 2:7–8; Heb. 2:10; 12:2–3). Perhaps the worst suffering was the shame He endured from people believing He had been rejected by the Father (Matt. 27:42–44). He kept choosing at each trial to entrust "Himself to Him who judges righteously" instead of justifying Himself (1 Pet. 2:23). Jesus' perfected human nature, fully joined to His divine nature, is within the believer as his new nature: complete in Christ and becoming complete in its expression through His disciple (Col. 2:10; 3:10).

21. God created first in heaven the prototype of every animal that ever lived on earth, and it still exists there in a perfect state (James 1:17; Heb. 8:5; 9:23). In the case of dinosaurs and other animals that ate meat on earth instead of the grass and plants that God provided for them (Gen. 1:30), they remain in heaven as the gentle, herbivorous creatures that He made them. He will restore the carnivorous animals now on earth to this condition during the Millennium (Isa. 11:6–9; Rom. 8:19–21).

22. Celestial beings have bodies of spirit instead of physical matter; therefore they are able to appear or disappear (Judg. 6:12, 21) or to change their outward appearance (Exod. 3:2) as needed. Many have spiritual

bodies that look like the physical form of human beings (Dan. 10:16, 18), but others are unique creations of God, as are the four living creatures around the throne in heaven (Rev. 4:6–8) or the wheels (Ezek. 1:15–20).

23. The Holy Spirit opposes the flesh in believers; He presses the power out of it in order that He may bring forth the obedience of Christ (Gal. 5:17; Rom. 8:12–13; Col. 3:5). The outward discipline that the Spirit custom designs for each of us is meant to bring us to accept God's "sentence of death within ourselves in order that we should not trust in ourselves, but in God who raises the dead" (2 Cor. 1:9; 4:10–11). This process is like pressing out the juice of grapes, leaving the "flesh" or pulp lifeless. Some Christians refuse to accept and carry this individual cross as Jesus continually bears His private cross (Matt. 16:24). Therefore they have to continue in chastisements from God for years (Heb. 12:5–6).

24. Children in human families learn to obey by being disciplined or trained by their parents, and so do the children of God. Divine discipline also is meant to bring us to receive the gift of repentance, so that we change our attitude and direction and return to peace and right relationship with our heavenly Father by sharing in His holiness (Heb. 12:10–11).

25. Sometimes angels must strongly oppose us, as the angel with the drawn sword blocked Balaam's path (Num. 22:22–35). An angel also wrestled with Jacob at the ford of the Jabbok (Gen. 32:24–31).

26. The heavenly host is watching how we believers on earth run the course of obedience in Christ Jesus (Heb. 12:1). When the sons of God are revealed in the last days as those who "will shine forth as the sun in the kingdom" (Matt. 13:43), "the whole creation," including the angels and the redeemed in heaven, will share in "the freedom of the glory of the children of God" (Rom. 8:18–19, 21–22; Col. 3:4). Christians have received "the promise" of the Spirit (Acts 2:39), who brings forth Christ as that "something better for us, so that apart from us they [the redeemed in heaven and the angels] should not be made perfect" (Heb. 11:39–40; 1 Pet. 1:10–11). All heaven also awaits the victory Jesus won over Satan and his host at Calvary to be enforced by the overcoming church, so that all of God's enemies will be cast out of that part of heaven that they occupy (Eph. 3:10; Rev. 12:10–12).

27. The Bible portrays the living church as the bride of Christ in graphically romantic terms in the Song of Solomon. An example is the Lord

speaking to her, "Arise, my darling, my beautiful one, and come along!...For your voice is sweet, and your form is lovely" (Song of Sol. 2:13–14). The prophets speak of God's affectionate love for His people (Jer. 2:2; Ezek. 16:8). Human marriage is a type and foreshadowing of Christ's love for His bride, the overcoming church (Eph. 5:25, 29–30), to whom He will be joined before He returns to earth with her to reign (Rev. 2:11, 26–27; 3:21; 19:7–9; 20:6).

# Chapter 8
## The Corrupted Strata

1. God's people are called sheep throughout the Bible, for they are utterly dependent upon the Lord, their Shepherd, for nourishment, discipline, and protection (John 10:9, 29). Jesus Christ is "Lord of all" (Acts 10:36) "by the exertion of the [resurrection] power that He has even to subject all things to Himself" (Phil. 3:21; Eph. 1:22). He proclaims His lordship right in the midst of Satan's headquarters by the sheepfold where "no one [can] snatch...out of [His] hand" any believer whom Christ brings there (John 10:28). The Lord leads them in and out of this place of safety in the presence of their worst enemies (Ps. 23:5; John 10:3–4). He is the one and only door that leads to life (John 10:9), "who opens and no one will shut, and who shuts and no one opens" (Rev. 3:7).

2. The command post for the devil's worldwide organization of demons and fallen angels is in a lower sphere (Eph. 6:12; 3:10; Col. 2:15; 1 Cor. 15:24). God's throne is in the third or highest heaven (2 Cor. 12:2; Eph. 4:10). From his headquarters, Satan governs a wicked empire on earth through lust, deception, and pride. The Bible calls this evil realm "the world" whenever it refers to the system of commerce, industry, finance, education, science, medicine, and law that makes man the measure of all things and omits God (1 John 2:15–16; James 4:4).

3. The shepherd's staff represents the Lord's authority and power (Exod. 14:16; 17:9, 11; Ps. 23:4).

4. Porpoise skin is water repellent and so served as the outer covering on the tent or tabernacle (Exod. 26:14). Nothing of the sin and death in Satan's domain is to touch the feet of the believer! The shoes are red, a witness to the victory over the devil and his host won through the blood sacrifice of Christ on Calvary (Col. 2:15). The shed blood of the Lamb not only overcomes any accusations of the enemy, but it also cleanses from any possible defilement through being in his loathsome territory (Rev. 12:17; 1 John 1:9; 2 Cor. 7:1).

5. Sin and death have brought physical darkness to Satan's territory in the midheaven (Col. 1:13). Because of the vicious hatred there, the inhabitants also walk in spiritual darkness (1 John 2:11), the opposite of the love that enables one to abide in the Light of God (1 John 1:5; 2:10).

6. The sources of this torment are the areas of human soul life (mind, emotions, and will) on earth that Satan and his demons control. Everyone is born with his soul faculties subject to the law of sin and death in his bodily members (Rom. 7:23), and hence he is dominated by "the [evil] spirit that is now working in the sons of disobedience" (Eph. 2:1–3). Satan therefore has a legal right to bring distress and suffering in every person's soul until that person believes in Christ Jesus. He is then joined to Him, submitting his soul faculties to the Lord as he begins to think, desire, and choose as He does. This is "the salvation of your souls" (Matt. 16:24–25; Luke 21:19; Heb. 10:39; James 1:21; 1 Pet. 1:9).

Satan's kingdom above ground includes the earth's surface (1 John 5:19), the atmosphere above the earth (Eph. 2:2; 6:12), and his head-quarters in a lower part of the heavenly realm or midheaven (Luke 10:18). All three of these areas are interconnected; whatever he controls in one area of his kingdom, he also controls in all the other areas.

7. In Leviticus 11 and Deuteronomy 14, God separates the animal kingdom into two categories: the clean and the unclean. The clean animals were offered in sacrifice on the altar and used as food for His people. The unclean ones were not so acceptable. It would seem that Satan and his demons select many of these unclean animals to inhabit, as the legion of evil spirits asked Jesus to send them into the pigs (Mark 5:12–13). The hideous bodies of some demons are the result of living in an atmosphere of utter corruption apart from the light, life, and love of God. There is a hierarchy of rank among demons. A slug-like animal represents the lowest order—those that crawl on their bellies (Gen. 3:14; Lev. 11:42).

8. The Father has so highly exalted the risen Christ "that at the name of Jesus every knee should bow, of those who are in heaven, and on earth, and under the earth" (Phil. 2:10). "Every knee" includes every creature in Satan's domain, too.

9. The filthy, stagnant water is a pitiful imitation of the crystal clear river of life in God's heaven (Rev. 22:1).

10. The crocodile is an example of a reptile that the ancient Egyptians worshiped as a god. This culture often made idols of animals they feared, like serpents and lions. They considered the crocodile to have godlike qualities. It is also the only animal without a tongue, which the ancients considered godlike. Furthermore, it is almost impenetrable and seemingly afraid of nothing.

11. God has compassion on the suffering of His children (Exod. 3:7; Deut. 30:3) and is hurt by their unfaithfulness (Hos. 11:8; Mic. 6:3). In direct contrast, Satan and his demons find pleasure in defiling the children of God (Rom. 1:32) and rejoice in their sins, which is the opposite of love (1 Cor. 13:6). The enemy host compounds hatred in their kingdom by taking delight in refusing to give any relief to those who are in pain (2 Tim. 3:3).

12. The fleshly use of a Christian's tongue is demonic, whether he is cursing others or attempting to speak wisdom (James 3:6, 9, 15). When he speaks out of his earthly self, he seeks his own glory and so gives Satan the right to use him (John 7:18). When we enjoy hearing of the fall of another into sin or slander each other or presume to pass judgment on the guilt of another, we are usurping God's place and are participating in Satan's sins (Rom. 14:10; James 4:11–12; Rev. 12:10). We are thereby withholding the blessing of God that we "were called" to give others (1 Pet. 3:9). We are even to "bless those who persecute [us]; bless and curse not" (Rom. 12:14). Christians have the great privilege of asking God for life for any brother or sister whom they see committing a sin (except sins for which the sinner deserves to die) (1 John 5:16).

13. The demons in Scripture found the presence of Jesus tormenting to them (Mark 5:7). "For everyone who does evil hates the light, and does not come to the light, lest his deeds should be exposed" (John 3:20). The true nature of "all things become[s] visible when they are exposed by the light" of God (Eph. 5:13). Since "God is light, and in Him there is no darkness at all," there can be no fellowship (but rather enmity) with Him for those who walk in darkness (1 John 1:5–6; Rom. 8:7).

14. All is damp or watery because satanic creatures fear the coming flames of hell (Matt. 8:29; Luke 8:31). Jesus said that they are even tormented by dry places on earth (Matt. 12:43). On one occasion thousands of demons who were in a person asked the Lord to send them into a herd of pigs so that they could go with the animals into the lake (Mark 5:12–13). The devil has long secured worship of himself on earth with sacred trees and tree trunks or pillars called Asherim that represent female deities of fertility (Deut. 16:21–22). These tree trunks are dead, as are all idols (Hab. 2:18–19).

15. Snakes or serpents are a major symbol for Satan and his demons in Scripture (Rev. 12:9; Luke 10:19). One reason is that God cursed the serpent in the Garden of Eden because it was used by the devil to

deceive Eve (Gen. 3:1, 14). Jesus said that Satan must maintain unity among those in his evil kingdom (Mark 3:24–26), a oneness built upon hatred of God and His creatures (John 15:25; Ps. 69:4).

16. All believers "were formerly darkness" before receiving the light of the nature of Christ Jesus within them (Eph. 5:8; 2 Cor. 4:6). Their old nature was darkness because they had grown into the image of their father, the devil (Matt. 13:38; John 8:41, 44; 1 John 3:8, 10). Remnants of their old, dark ways of thinking, desiring, choosing, and acting may remain unnoticed if Christians continue to rely only upon their natural observation and perception. To perceive only the things of this world admits the old darkness again (Matt. 6:22–23; 2 Cor. 4:4). Their spiritual eyes need to be enlightened to the reality of Christ and be focused on Him (Eph. 1:18–19; Heb. 12:2). Of course, anything the believer does secretly with a guilty or doubtful conscience is hidden away from the light of fellowship with Jesus (1 John 1:6). We are to walk before the Lord with nothing in our lives concealed from Him (Eph. 5:11–12). Everything is continually exposed to let His presence cleanse and transform all into His light (Eph. 5:13–14; 1 John 1:7).

17. Satan has counterfeited all the things in heaven that are possible to him, an example being his guise as an angel of light (2 Cor. 11:14). Above all else, he craves to be worshiped (Matt. 4:8–9). Praise and homage come to Satan's temple from the great multitude of idolatrous places of worship throughout the world by means of the demons who inspire this worship (1 Cor. 10:20; Rev. 9:20). The worship of false gods even infiltrated the first temple in Jerusalem during the reign of many kings of Judah (2 Kings 23:4; Ezek. 8:9–16). The first recorded instance of satanic worship occurred in Babylon around 2150 B.C. A rebellious host of people erected a tower whose "top reach[ed] into heaven," meaning that the devilish signs of the false zodiac were used for divination there (Gen. 11:4). The antediluvian patriarchs knew the true meaning of these constellations of stars, for God tells the story in the night sky of salvation in Jesus Christ (Gen. 1:14 ["signs"]; Ps. 19:1–2).

18. A horn symbolizes the power of a king or kingdom for good or evil (Rev. 5:6; 12:3). Satan undergirds heathen kings on earth to increase their treasuries of silver and gold, which the Bible calls "treasures of darkness, and hidden wealth of secret places" (Isa. 45:3). He increases their earthly wealth in exchange for their homage and praise through false gods (Isa. 65:11). In the first temple in Jerusalem, there were "upper rooms" called "treasuries" (2 Chron. 3:9; 2 Kings

12:18). Gold and silver that had been dedicated to the Lord for His purposes were stored in these rooms. These treasures came as gifts from the king or wealthy people and from the spoils of war (1 Kings 7:51; 1 Chron. 29:6–7; Num. 31:48–54; 2 Sam. 8:9–12). At times the kings of Judah gave these treasures away to try to gain military protection from enemies instead of relying upon God (1 Kings 15:18–19).

19. The valuables taken as spoil from enemies of the Israelites in war had to be purified either by fire or by water (Num. 31:21–23). A time is coming when everything belonging to God that Satan has stolen will be released from his headquarters, then cleansed and restored to the highest heaven (Heb. 9:23; 2 Pet. 3:12–13; Rev. 21:1, 5).

20. Not only will the stolen treasures be cleansed and returned to God, but the very terrain will be completely purified from the effects of darkness, sin, and death (as in the natural, see Ezekiel 36:6, 8–9, 13–15). The Father will signal the beginning of His judgment on all of Satan's host by raising His sword and by severing all that is His from the enemy (Deut. 32:41; Ps. 7:12; Heb. 12:26–27; Hag. 2:21–22; Zeph. 3:8).

21. "All fat is the LORD'S" (along with the blood) of the animal sacrifices on the brazen altar, "an offering by fire for a soothing aroma" (Lev. 3:16–17). God commanded this from the beginning with Adam, Eve, and their sons (Gen. 4:4). Animal fat burned on the altar symbolizes nourishment and fragrance to the Father (Ezek. 44:7; Lev. 4:31). It represents the "sacrifice of praise" that is "continually offer[ed] up" (Heb. 13:15) through the Son (Acts 2:33) by the fire of the Holy Spirit (Lev. 3:3–5) from the people of God (Acts 2:3–4, 11). The Father seeks such worshipers (John 4:23). The main purpose of fat is to be "burned" (oxidized) to produce energy. The physical fat of the animal sacrifices was removed from organs in the abdominal cavity, which is the location in Christians of the human spirit from which praise and worship proceeds (John 7:38).

The fat (and the blood), God's portion of the sacrifices, was offered first on the altar—before the rest of the animal—in order to rise in smoke toward heaven (1 Sam. 2:15–16; Lev. 4:34–35). Likewise, the first order in approaching the throne of God in spirit is to "enter…His courts with praise" (Ps. 100:4; 96:8). As fat is that which abounds, believers are to abound in praise to our God. The word *fat* is an expression used to designate the best part, for example, "living on the fat of the land." Praise to God is surely the best part for human beings (Ps. 147:1). When we worship anything of the earthly realm, we violate the first two commandments and allow demons to capture this spiritual fat.

22. Nothing that is not of God will be able to stand before His divine light, for "the powers of the heavens will be shaken" (Matt. 24:29; Isa. 34:4; Mark 4:22; Eph. 5:13).

23. A drone or monotonous tone in ritual incantation is used in some heathen worship to contact the power of the spirit world. The Lord expressly rejected the use of such mantras (Matt. 6:7).

24. Israel is often compared to a female (Isa. 54:5–6; Hos. 2:14, 16, 19–20). So is the church as the bride of Christ (Song of Sol. 4:8–10; Rev. 19:7). God designed human marriage on earth to prepare the two mates for eternal marriage to Jesus Christ (Eph. 5:25–27, 31–32; Rev. 21:9). The church is the spiritual womb in which the children of God are conceived, born, and reared (Song of Sol. 8:5; Rev. 12:1–2, 5). From the earliest days Satan has perverted this sacred imagery into licentious worship of female deities of fertility. In all the nature religions of history, there have been "mother goddesses" (Acts 19:27; 1 Kings 11:5). The Bible often calls this idol "the queen of heaven" (Jer. 7:18; 44:17–19). During many periods Israel worshiped "the Baals and the Ashtaroth" (Judg. 10:6; 1 Sam. 12:10). The idolatrous church in these last days is pictured as a harlot queen called "Babylon the Great." She is ruled by demonic powers just as the first Babylon in Genesis 11:4, 9 was ruled by them (Rev. 17:1, 4–5). She is foretold in Isaiah 47:1, 7–9.

25. Israel has been a captive nation in political terms and in spiritual chains for most of her history (Ps. 106:41–42; Isa. 52:2). Many present Christians have been "conformed to this world" system (Rom. 12:2). They are caught in "the snare of the devil, having been held captive by him to do his will" (2 Tim. 2:26). The captive church ensnares her converts with an illusion of grandeur—prosperous, outward appearance—and activities that are actually "dead works" and "devoid of the Spirit" (Heb. 9:14; Jude 19). This worldly church chains her members by teaching them to idolize the religious organization and by binding them to perpetuate it through traditional and rote forms of worship (John 11:48; Isa. 29:13).

26. Everything about the evil one and his kingdom is false and an imitation of the true (John 8:44). The true fire of God "burns up the chaff" in believers and ignites the new heart to become a living flame of love for God (Matt. 3:12; Song of Sol. 8:6). The false fire of the enemy

merely torments and destroys (John 15:6; Rev. 9:17–18). Honey at times represents the false comfort that Satan provides through the fleshly church: smooth, sweet words based on earthly wisdom that is soulish and demonic like the words of an adulteress (Prov. 5:3; James 3:15).

27. King Solomon built a magnificent throne of ivory and gold, like no other throne on earth (2 Chron. 9:17–19). Furthermore, "he went up to the house of the LORD" by a stairway of such grandeur that it took the visiting Queen of Sheba's breath away (2 Chron. 9:3–4). His love of opulence was a root from which grew other idolatrous sins. Satan will give the coming Antichrist the power and authority of his throne to use on the earth (Rev. 13:2).

28. An evil "spirit of divination" spoke through a slave girl in Acts 16:16 to foretell the future. The Greek word for *divination* means "python." Python was the name of a mythical serpent that guarded the Delphic oracle where secret knowledge was thought to be revealed. God forbids the evil art of people who seek to discover knowledge about the future that He Himself has not revealed to them (Deut. 18:10–11). The devil cooperates with this ungodly practice and supplies some of his limited knowledge if it will suit his purposes. Psychics, astrologists, fortunetellers, and adherents of the so-called New Age religion use modern divination.

29. God on His throne in heaven is attended by the redeemed "from every tribe and tongue and people and nation" (Rev. 5:9–10). In evil imitation, Satan's court is composed of ruling, fallen angels known as "princes" (Dan. 10:12–13, 20). These angels control the heathen rulers, nations, and areas throughout the earth for the devil's purposes and bring their homage to Satan's throne (Rev. 17:1–2, 15).

30. Through consorting with Satan's evil, spiritual empire on earth, which the Bible calls "the world" (Matt. 4:8; John 14:30), the false church receives the "bodies and souls of men" (Rev. 18:13, NIV) whom she holds on to for display. God calls her the Esau church because she cares more for her comfort, gratification, and convenience than for her spiritual birthright (Gen. 25:29–34).

31. All along God has sent true prophets to speak for Him to His people, but time and time again they have been rejected in favor of false prophets who prophesy by means of an evil spirit what the people want to hear (Jer. 2:8; 23:13–17, 25–32). Jesus said that false prophets would arise in the last days "to mislead, if possible, even the elect" (Matt. 24:24).

32. The devil is able to perform signs (miracles) and wonders (marvels) through his human servants on earth. He did this, up to a certain point, through Jannes and Jambres, the magicians of Pharaoh's court (Exod. 7:11–12, 20–22; 8:5–7, 18; 2 Tim. 3:8). Simon the magician astonished the people of Samaria with his diabolical arts (Acts 8:9–11). In the last days, Jesus said that people in whom Satan is working will show "great signs and wonders" (Matt. 24:24; 2 Thess. 2:9–11; Rev. 13:13–15).

33. There were female and male cult prostitutes during periods of Israel's history (1 Kings 14:24). Along the outer walls of Solomon's temple in the three stories of side rooms that were built for the priests on duty, there was cult prostitution at times (2 Kings 23:7; Hos. 4:14). The fallen church has committed adultery through her friendship with the world system masterminded by the devil, adopting many of its values and methods, thereby making herself "an enemy of God" (James 4:4; Rev. 17:1–2; 18:3, 9).

34. In the last years before Christ returns, the corrupt church will be in league with Satan's Antichrist (Rev. 12:3; 13:1; 17:3, 7). This human beast and his armies will turn and destroy her with fire in one day (Rev. 17:16). God executes this judgment against her for "corrupting the earth with her immorality, and He has avenged the blood of His bond-servants on her" (Rev. 19:2). The "cup of demons" is that which sustains them (1 Cor. 10:21). With Christians it is the cup of Christ's blood (1 Cor. 11:25). With Satan's host it is the "cup full of abominations and of the unclean things of her immorality" (Rev. 17:4).

35. The fleshly church will "become a dwelling place of demons and a prison of every unclean spirit" (Rev. 18:2) when God completely withdraws the light of the Spirit from her (2 Thess. 2:7, 11). God will separate out the true and living church of His Son (Rev. 18:4; Isa. 52:11; Jer. 51:6). This emerging church has only one standard by which she measures everything: Christ Jesus. The true Christians will allow the fire of God's Spirit to burn up everything that is not of Christ in them and in their lives. The members of the false church will not allow the fire to deal with the ungodly use of their bodies and their natural self life (the flesh) or their love for the things of Satan's evil system (the world). The enemy will still have access to them. The Lord says in this vision, "Many will go with her [the false church]." Many of those who call themselves Christians will remain with the spiritually dead church. As in all past generations, only a remnant will be saved (Isa. 10:20–22; Zech. 8:12; Matt. 7:13–14).

# Chapter 9
## Bowels of the Dragon

1. Among the laws given by God to the Israelites was one that required them to have bowel movements outside the camp, digging a hole and covering up the excrement. They were to keep the camp clean and sanitary, for the holy God walked in the midst of His people (Deut. 23:12–14). In his headquarters, Satan deliberately defies the laws of God, particularly the laws concerning His purity and holiness. Within the tunnel there were foul odors of feces; the evil host enjoys being indecent and defiling the lower part of the heavens to which God has assigned them for a time. This is one of the reasons why Scripture calls demons "unclean spirits" (Mark 5:13).

2. At times the Lord allows the thick darkness from the enemy to come upon the believer, together with a limited assault by demons. This is not an unloving thing for Him to do; it is necessary for us to experience the hideous depth of corruption in the flesh (Gal. 5:19–21; 2 Tim. 3:2–5). This pollution is ever present, together with Christ's victory in us over the power of the flesh (Gal. 5:24). The Spirit tests everyone (as Jesus was tried in the wilderness) before they are given added responsibilities. The flesh, our worst enemy, is the earthly expression of the old, outer person who was born captive to the law of sin and death within (Rom. 7:23; Eph. 2:3). Evil spirits have helped fashion this natural person into the image and likeness of Satan during the years before we came to Christ (Eph. 2:1–2; John 8:44).

   The flesh is a storehouse of memories, attitudes, and emotions stemming from the resentments, injustices, and pain we have experienced in the past. The reason these are still with us is because the flesh cannot forgive or love, anymore than the devil can forgive or love. Demons can tap this reservoir of hatred within us at a moment's notice if God or the believer allows it. The flesh cannot love anyone but itself, for it hates God, the source of love (Rom. 8:6–7; 1 John 4:7–8). It will always be in bondage to the law of sin and death (Rom. 7:18, 23–24). The flesh cannot be redeemed. It will remain bound by sin for the duration of one's earthly life, as it cannot repent (Heb. 12:17).

   Victory over the power of the flesh was won by Christ on the cross when the old, corporate heart (the power source of the flesh) of the human race died with Him there (Ezek. 36:26; Rom. 6:6; 2 Cor. 5:21; Col. 3:3). When He rose from death and ascended to the Father, a new inner person of heart and spirit in the likeness of Jesus' resurrected heart and spirit became available to set every believer free from the dominion of the flesh (Eph. 4:24; Col. 3:10; 1 Pet. 3:4; Ezek. 36:26–27; Rom. 8:2; 1 Cor. 6:17). The love of Christ now has the power to control us rather than the flesh (2 Cor. 5:14; Phil. 3:21).

We must be brought to hate our flesh and every expression of it (Jude 23; Luke 14:26; John 12:25). We are to put no confidence in ourselves but in Him who raises the dead (2 Cor. 1:9). God gradually reveals to us the depth of the hideousness of our flesh (Gal. 5:19–21; Col. 3:5, 8). He reveals it so that we may vehemently oppose it in the power of the Holy Spirit (Rom. 8:13; 13:14; Gal. 5:17, 24). We also may remain hidden within Christ, trusting His presence to be all that every situation requires in the Father's eyes (Col. 3:3; Phil. 4:6–7).

As we live on Christ's level and share all things with Him in loving submission to His needs, His presence in us will meet our needs and the needs of others (Ps. 16:11; Phil. 4:19).

3. This was the same cry of another person who was in darkness: the blind beggar Bartimaeus (Mark 10:46–47). The Spirit helps us to counterattack the enemy with the spoken word of Scripture, as He helped Jesus on earth (Matt. 4:4; Eph. 6:17; Rev. 12:11).

4. Angels strengthened Jesus in His trials (Matt. 4:11; Luke 22:43). Second Thessalonians 3:3 says, "The Lord is faithful, and He will strengthen and protect you from the evil one." (See also John 17:15; Ephesians 3:16; Philippians 4:13; Hebrews 2:18; 1 Peter 5:10). No human being can possibly survive the full assault of the enemy, but the Lord sets limits to the severity of a trial (Job 1:12; 2:6).

5. This world system based upon earthly pleasure, gain, and glory was offered by its ruler, Satan, to Jesus in His temptations in the wilderness (Matt. 4:8–9). To love the world system is to love its prince and to be without the love of God in oneself (James 4:4; 1 John 2:15–16; Luke 16:13). Jesus gained the victory over Satan's kingdom on this earth on the cross. The world system was crucified (separated by death) to us and we to the world (Gal. 6:14; John 12:31; 15:19). When resurrected in spirit with Christ Jesus (Eph. 2:5–6; Col. 3:1), the life of the redeemed is "far above all rule and authority and power and dominion" of the enemy (Eph. 1:21). Jesus will manifest in us His overcoming of the world (John 16:33; Rev. 3:21).

6. Joshua admonished the children of Israel to choose between serving the false gods of this world or serving the living God (Josh. 24:14–15). The greater Joshua, Jesus Christ, said that a person cannot

live for God and also live for the world: "No one can serve two masters" (Matt. 6:24).

7. The basic sin of Lucifer in heaven was arrogant presumption in claiming God's giftings and grace to him as his own to be used to make himself like God (Isa. 14:14; Ezek. 28:17; 1 Tim. 3:6). The presumptuous sin of the Israelites in the desert was passing judgment on God for not being faithful in providing for them (Exod. 17:7). In the wilderness Satan brought a temptation against Jesus to be presumptuous and put God the Father to the test by requiring Him to prove His faithfulness (Luke 4:9–12).

   Pride in its most heinous form is the effrontery of overstepping the bounds of the dependent creature so as to presume to judge God and others (Gen. 3:5; Num. 11:1, 5–6; 21:4–6; Matt. 7:1–2; James 4:11–12; 5:9). Satan could find no pride in Jesus (John 14:30). When He suffered unjustly, He did not retaliate but "kept entrusting Himself to [His Father] who judges righteously" (1 Pet. 2:23).

   Believers hold their position in Christ, clothed in His victory over the enemy, to resist being moved from that place of His triumph (Heb. 2:14–15; Col. 2:15; 2 Cor. 2:14). Unmoved by the schemes of the enemy, we stand firm and proclaim the Word of Scripture as supplied by the Spirit (Eph. 6:11, 13, 17).

   It was necessary for Jesus to have complete victory over the enemy during His forty days of fasting in the desert in order that He might then return to Galilee "in the power of the Spirit" (Luke 4:14). All believers need to experience the power of Christ's triumph within them so that they might become steadfast during any proving of Christ's faith in them that God allows the devil to bring (James 1:2–4). In this way they can begin to reign with the Lord even in this present life (James 1:12; Rom. 5:17; Rev. 2:10; 3:10–11).

8. When believers are tested by trials or temptations, it is for the purpose of having Christ's own faith within them tested in order to demonstrate to them its genuineness (James 1:2–4; 1 Pet. 1:7). We have nothing of our own with which to pass these tests. Jesus' faith was perfected through His suffering every trial we may face and His remaining obedient to His Father (Heb. 2:18; 4:15; 5:8–9).

   Our part is to obey Him by trusting Him as our victory; His part is to be that obedience in us that is necessary to demonstrate His victory in our present testing. We must not rely upon anything of ourselves to obey God. To clearly teach us this truth, Jesus gave one commandment that He called "My commandment": to love others just as He loved us (John 13:34). It is, of course, humanly impossible for us to love as He loves. To establish this truth even more firmly, Paul added two more humanly unattainable commands: to forgive one another just as the Lord forgave you (Eph. 4:32; Col. 3:13), and to accept one another just as Christ accepted us (Rom. 15:7). Jesus must be that love, forgiveness, and acceptance of others; He must be all things unto us (1 Cor. 1:30; Col. 3:11). He said, "As the Father has sent Me, I also send you [into the world]" (John 17:18; 20:21).

9. In times of temptation, we are to proclaim to the devil and his demons that Jesus Christ is our victory over them, for we died with Him on Calvary and now share His risen life (Gal. 2:20; Col. 3:3).

10. The word *brimstone* in Scripture means "sulphur." Sulphur is a yellow solid that becomes a liquid when its temperature rises, and it burns with a suffocating odor. It is part of the molten rock called magma that is in the mantle or layer that extends some eighteen hundred miles beneath the earth's crust. Hence sulphur is found plentifully in volcanic regions. Burning sulphur is poured out from heaven by God in judgment upon the sins of mankind (Gen. 19:24; Ezek. 38:22). The abyss or "bottomless pit" deep within the earth is a prison for the most evil spirits, who will be loosed in the last days to spew burning sulphur from their mouths against unrepentant humanity (Rev. 9:18). Sulphur oozes from beneath Satan's palace as a constant reminder from God that his house is built upon that which cannot stand (Luke 6:49). It is also a reminder that his final place of abode will be the lake of burning sulphur in hell (Rev. 19:20).

11. Dragons in Satan's kingdom are not imaginary or mythical creatures. They are demons with serpentine bodies (serpents being venomous reptiles) that have grown to be monsters. The principal Hebrew word meaning "dragon" is *tannin,* which is also translated "serpent" and "sea monster" (Ps. 74:13; Isa. 27:1; 34:14). The root of the Hebrew *tannin* is the word *tan,* which means "jackal," a wild dog that often subsists on the remains of animals slaughtered by other carnivores. Another Hebrew word used to describe dragons is *saraph,* translated as "fiery serpent" (Deut. 8:15). It is the same Hebrew word that is also translated "seraphim," the plural of seraph, who are an order of fiery, heavenly beings stationed above God's throne (Isa. 6:2). As the blessed seraphim burn with the holiness of God, so the fiery, serpentine dragons are diabolical fiends that have grown to resemble the character of the evil one whom they guard. In the Bible the words *dragon, serpent,* or *sea monster* are also used as figures of speech to describe the literal, bloodthirsty ferocity of Satan or the heathen kings and nations that he controls (Rev. 12:4; 13; Ezek. 32:2).

12. Mountains in Scripture are often symbolic of kingdoms. Again in imitation of heaven, the devil has erected his dwelling place on a mountain, for God dwells on Mount Zion (Ps. 2:6; 9:11; Heb. 12:22; Rev. 14:1). "Out of Zion, the perfection of beauty, God has shown forth" in radiant splendor (Ps. 50:2). The plan of the evil one was to set up his throne in heaven above all the other angels and to reign there like God (Isa. 14:13–14). Such was the utter folly of his deluded mind, corrupted by arrogance and ambition (Ezek. 28:17; James 3:14).

13. Satan's palace is more like a castle, which means a large and stately residence that is fortified against an enemy. It is also a palace in the sense that such mansions are usually where kings live. We see the devil's dwelling reflected in the palace of the king of Babylon, whereby they both claimed the power and the glory for themselves (Dan. 4:28–30). There are no palaces or castles in heaven, for God does not seclude Himself in a castle—He has nothing to fear from His enemies (2 Chron. 6:18; Ps. 2:1–5). The devil, on the other hand, rules by fear, lies, and torture; he must isolate himself in his head-quarters and surround himself with guards.

14. In classical mythology, a harpy was a winged monster with the head and upper torso of a woman and the lower body and claws of a vul-ture. This predatory creature was very fierce, starved-looking, and loathsome. It lived in an atmosphere of filth and stench, contami-nating everything it came near. These harpy angels that protect Satan are a supreme example of once beautiful creatures who dwelt in the light of God's presence in heaven but chose to follow the evil one into utter degradation. A dreadful example of this type of demonic crea-ture is described in Revelation 9:7–10.

15. Satan is consumed with hate for God and therefore with hate for His children. Since the day the evil one deceived Eve, his strategy has been to corrupt the church in order to make void the working out of the cross of Christ (Gen. 3:15). His bitter enmity is focused upon the Son of God who humbled Himself to be born as a human being, to die as a common criminal, and to carry His perfected human nature into heaven. The Lord's goal is to grant to anyone who receives Him the right to share both His human and divine natures forever. It must have been very difficult for this supremely beau-tiful, wise, and blameless cherub, who was one of the guardians surrounding the Father (Ezek. 28:13–14), to accept His plan: to make mere earthly people a part of Himself and fellow heirs of all that He had given to His Son (John 17: 21–23; 3:35; Rom. 8:17). To have mortal human beings advance to intimate union with God

beyond what he could ever know (1 Pet. 1:12) and to have these adopted children share in Christ's reign over him and the other angels (Rev. 20:4; 22:5) must have been a humbling he could not accept (Ezek. 28:17; 1 Tim. 3:6).

16. Ezekiel 28:12–19 tells us more about Lucifer than any other Scripture (the name given him in Isaiah 14:12, KJV). In Ezekiel 28:14, the Holy Spirit reveals that he was "the anointed cherub who covers [or guards]." He was the highest of several cherubim who surrounded the Father continually as a kind of honor guard to His radiant glory (Ezek. 9:3; 10:18).

17. The other main Scripture that describes Lucifer's fall is Isaiah 14:12–15. In verse 13, he aspired to sit upon a throne that would be elevated above all the other angels, who are called "the stars of God." Other examples of the Scriptures describing angels as stars are in Revelation 8:10 and 9:1–2. In truth, Lucifer was the most gifted and glorious of the heavenly host, but God so endowed him in order that he might better honor God and serve others rather than exalt himself.

18. God declared the raven to be an unclean bird (Lev. 11:15). Noah sent it from the ark to determine the extent to which the water had subsided (Gen. 8:6–7). Being a carrion eater, the bird may have subsisted on dead carcasses and did not return to Noah. The bird's name has become the source of words such as *ravenous,* a word meaning "rapacious" (seizing by violence) and "voracious" (devouring). No wonder the evil one chose to take the form of this darksome bird. Good angels can change their appearance (Gen. 18:1–2; 19:1) and so can Satan, since after his defection he retained his former rank and giftings in corrupted forms (2 Cor. 11:14; Rom. 11:29).

19. Satan here mocks the Lord by simply calling Him "Jesus of Nazareth." The unclean spirit in the synagogue used these words to Him (Mark 1:24). The words "Jesus the Nazarene" were part of the inscription that the devil moved Pilate to write in derision and have placed on the cross (John 19:19). In those days to say that a person was a Nazarene was a term of reproach (John 1:46).

20. Lucifer once walked in closest fellowship "in the midst of the stones of fire," which means intimacy within the very heart of the Father (Ezek. 28:14). The Bible speaks of the fire of God (Ezek. 1:4, 27). At that time Lucifer loved the Son of God very deeply, but now as Satan, he has only absolute hatred for the Lamb of God who denied Himself in being born as a human being and in submitting in love to the

# Notes

Father unto death on a cross: the complete opposite of the arrogant presumption of Satan.

21. The human offspring of fallen angels who mated with earthly women are called Nephilim, which means "fallen ones." (In Genesis 6:2–4; Job 1:6; 2:1, "sons of God" are angels, creatures brought into being directly by God and not born.) They were later known by the names of Rephaim, Zuzim, Zamzummin, Emim, and Anakim. These were people of monstrous size and wickedness as they were truly children of Satan (Gen. 6:11–13). The flood became necessary to preserve the human race from being completely corrupted by these abnormal human beings (Gen. 6:5, 7; 2 Pet. 2:4–5; Jude 6).

    The "giants" here represent modern people of renown and great gifting, especially those in the fields of science and technology, who are able to cause the earth to tremble in awe at their natural knowledge and power to accomplish wonders. "Mountains" in Scripture are sometimes symbols of monumental obstacles or problems (Zech. 4:7; Matt. 17:20). Modern science seems capable of overcoming any earthly obstacle. When Christ returns to rule the earth, His almighty power will cause "mountains" to melt away (Mic. 1:3–4; Ps. 97:5). Nothing can stand before His presence, but all must bow to His authority as Lord of all (Mal. 3:2; Acts 10:36; Phil. 2:10).

    Giants also represent powerful fallen angels who will be loosed by Satan as we move toward the end (Rev. 9:1–11). Even the most powerful of the enemy's forces cannot stand before the power of our God.

22. A plumbline is a cord with a weight on one end; it is used in building construction to test whether something is perfectly vertical. It is used figuratively in Scripture of God's action in measuring the uprightness or vertical dimension of His people (His "building," 1 Cor. 3:9). The major scripture for God's dropping the plumbline to earth is Amos 7:7–8, where the apostate northern kingdom of Israel does not measure up to God's standard; the Lord "will spare them no longer." He destined this northern kingdom for destruction, with the people carried away into exile and scattered into oblivion (Amos 9:10; 2 Kings 17:5–6, 20, 23).

23. Twice in the history of the Israelites, God determined to destroy them completely and to begin again to build a new nation with Moses as its leader (Exod. 32:10, 14; Num. 14:11–12, 20). At Moses' intercession, the Lord relented by granting mercy instead of strict justice.

24. Consuming fire is a part of God's being (Heb. 12:29). It is one expression of His holy love for His Son (John 3:35). His fiery love is

both zealous and jealous (Exod. 20:5; Deut. 4:24; Ezek. 36:5; Zeph. 3:8). There is a good and godly jealousy (2 Cor. 11:2). Both words convey the passionate ardor of the Father's heart to see His Son reproduced in His adopted children and manifested in all creation (2 Cor. 4:10–12; Num. 14:21). The fire of God's love is part of His glory (Exod. 24:17; 33:18–19; 34:6–7). The fire of His glory purifies and transforms His repentant and obedient children (Matt. 3:11–12; Mal. 3:2–3; 2 Cor. 3:18). It sets their hearts aflame as a living sacrifice (2 Chron. 7:1; Song of Sol. 8:6), "an offering by fire as a soothing aroma" (Num. 29:13). But for the unrepentant and rebellious, the fire of His unrequited love brings judgment (Isa. 66:15–17; Ps. 97:3; 1 Thess. 1:7–9; Heb. 10:26–27).

25. Edom is the nation that descended from Esau, Jacob's older brother (Gen. 25:24–26). Esau founded Edom, a word derived from a root meaning "red," which represents the color of the earth from which the human body was formed (Gen. 25:30; 36:1, 8–9). It also spiritually denotes a fleshly person rather than a spiritual one (1 Cor. 3:1, 3). The Edomites showed no mercy to the people of Judah when the latter were defeated and led into exile (Ps. 137:7; Obad. 10). Therefore they are the only neighboring country to God's people that was not given any promise of mercy from the Lord. They disappeared from history in A.D. 70 (Isa. 34:5, 10). As God stretched over Edom "the plumb line of emptiness" and "desolation" (Isa. 34:11), so it will be with the church of Edom in this closing period. God will withdraw all light from her; she will be in total spiritual darkness and be destroyed by fire (Isa. 60:2; Jer. 13:16; Joel 2:1–2; Rev. 17:16).

26. The church of Esau (or Edom) lives by natural wisdom and energy instead of taking one step at a time by the leading of the Holy Spirit (Gal. 5:16, 25). As Esau sold his birthright as the firstborn son to his brother, Jacob, for a bowl of lentil stew and bread, so the Esau church of today is controlled by the worldly spirit of immediate gratification and glory. She has no heart for the things of the Spirit (Rom. 8:7–8). The idolatries of the outward appearance of success and of recognition by man have replaced the desire for the hidden life in Christ (Matt. 6:1; Col. 3:3; Rev. 17:4; 18:7).

27. Already the separation of the servants of Christ from the idolatrous, unbelieving church has begun. The holy people of God are commanded: "Come out of her, my people, that you may not participate in her sins and that you may not receive of her plagues;... for...in one day...she will be burned up with fire" (Rev. 18:4, 8). At the instigation of Satan, Nimrod originally instituted this false religion at

# Notes

Babylon (Gen. 10:9–10; 11:4, 9). It substitutes a god made in the image of man for the God of the Bible. This substitution is done together with the practice of good works that gain merit for the worshipers (known in Scripture as "the works of their own hands," Jer. 1:16).

28. "For it is time for judgment to begin with the household of God" (1 Pet. 4:17; Heb. 10:30–31). God does not hold the pagan world primarily responsible for the deception that abounds; He holds the church accountable, for salvation in Christ is through His body, the church (Mark 16:15–16; Eph. 1:22; 3:10). Unless the church is manifesting the life of God and proclaiming His Word, there is no hope for those who do not obey the gospel of God (Eph. 2:12).

29. The righteous church will suffer great persecution in the last days by the corrupt church being in league with the world system of Satan (Rev. 17:3, 6). The redeemed and the angelic host will declare with one mighty voice in heaven: "Hallelujah!…He has judged the great harlot who was corrupting the earth with her immorality, and He has avenged the blood of His bondservants on her" (Rev. 19:1–2). "All the arrogant and every evildoer will be chaff; and the day that is coming will set them ablaze;…But for you who fear My name, the sun of righteousness will rise with healing in its wings" (Mal. 4:1–3; Isa. 60:1–3, 19).

30. The righteous church will see "the mountain [kingdom] of the Lord" established on earth after Christ returns. These saints will join with the "loud voices in heaven, saying, 'The kingdom of the world has become the kingdom of our Lord, and of His Christ; and He will reign forever and ever…Thou hast taken Thy great power and hast begun to reign'" (Rev. 11:15, 17).

31. God's children who overcome His enemies and learn to live above in Christ are promised "hidden manna" that will nourish them, food from heaven about which the world does not know (John 4:32; Rev. 2:17). They will "walk the streets of gold" in the celestial Jerusalem while still alive on earth, meaning that their inner person will live in Christ's realm (John 14:3; 17:24; 1 John 1:3; Heb. 12:22–24).

32. Satan inserted the thought in Eve's mind that she was more righteous than God, who was not respecting her rights (Gen. 3:4–5). Job "justified himself before [more than] God" (Job 32:2; 35:2), saying, "I am righteous, but God has taken away my right" (Job 34:5). God reproved him with the words: "Will you condemn Me that you may be justified?" (Job 40:8). God is the only one who has rights.

33. Christ Jesus has been made the throne of God, that is, the authority and power for the universe in His person (Isa. 22:23; Heb. 1:3; Col. 1:17). He is coming to "sit on His glorious throne [to exercise that dominion]" (Matt. 25:31; 28:18; Eph. 1:20–22; Rev. 3:21).

34. "Flesh and blood [that which is of the earth] cannot inherit the kingdom of God; nor does the perishable inherit the imperishable" (1 Cor. 15:50). That which stems from the natural person is cursed (Gen. 4:11; Jer. 17:5; Gal. 3:10). "Christ is all in all" in His kingdom (Col. 3:11), and only that which is of Him passes through God's flame (Rom. 15:18; 1 Cor. 3:11–15; 2 Cor. 3:5).

35. The Holy Spirit must bring all those in the kingdom of Christ to the full measure of development found in Jesus by their "grow[ing] up in all aspects into Him, who is the head" (Eph. 4:13, 15). He is the "precious corner stone" of God's house, the stone to which the Spirit aligns everything else (1 Pet. 2:5–6).

# Chapter 10
## The Throne of God

1. Paul speaks of "the third heaven," which Nehemiah calls "the heaven of heavens," which is the place of God's throne, His dwelling place (2 Cor. 12:2; Neh. 9:6; Ps. 11:4; 2 Chron. 6:33).

2. The floor of the throne room looks like "a sea of glass," clear as crystal (Rev. 4:6; 1:22, 26; Exod. 24:10). The angels and the redeemed there may stand or move about on this great expanse created of light from the Father (Rev. 15:2).

3. The Bible enjoins the redeemed on earth and in heaven, as well as the angels, to praise God with dancing (Ps. 149:3; 150:4). King David certainly obeyed the injunction (2 Sam. 6:14). Devotional group dancing in an orderly manner was part of the worship of God in ancient Israel (Exod. 15:20–21) and in the earliest centuries of the Christian church. In the fourth century, the bishop of Caesarea wrote: "Could there be anything more blessed than to imitate on earth the ring dance of the angels?" The courante originated in the sixteenth century as a lively, folk dance with quick, running steps. Singing to the Lord has always been a major part of praise on earth and in heaven (Ps. 47:6; Rev. 14:3). The biblical psalms were written to be sung (Ps. 47:7; Eph. 5:19).

4. Paul says that his spirit is able to pray or to sing by the working of the Holy Spirit within him (1 Cor. 14:14–15). The same Holy Spirit who is able to speak through believers on earth (1 Cor. 12:3, 7, 11) is also able to give the same song and the same dance movements to the multitude of the redeemed in heaven at the same time (Rev. 14:1, 3). This is possible because the unity of the Holy Spirit (1 Cor. 12:13; Rom. 8:14) with their spirits (1 Cor. 6:17) is pure and unobstructed, so that the Spirit flows freely to all. An example of this is in Revelation 5:13, when "every created thing which is in heaven" was saying the same words of praise to God.

5. *Epaggelias* is the Greek word that means "promises."

6. The hosts in heaven are able to see us on earth and rejoice over every sinner whom God saves (Luke 15:7; Heb. 12:1; Rev. 18:20; 19:1–2).

7. Of the three annual feasts appointed by God for all males in Israel—the Feast of Unleavened Bread, the Feast of the Harvest (first fruits), and the Feast of the Ingathering (Exod. 23:14–17)—only the last one is yet to be fulfilled in Christ. Known also as the Feast of Booths, as in Leviticus 23:34, the Feast of the Ingathering occurred each year at the close of the growing season when the final harvest of produce was made before winter (Lev. 23:39). It became the most important and joyous of the three feasts in the presence of the Lord (Exod. 34:23; Deut. 16:13–15). This last ingathering with respect to the celebration will begin to take place with the fullest outpouring of the Holy Spirit ever to occur, known as the "latter rain" (Joel 2:23, 28–29). There will be a great harvest, for "whoever calls on the name of the Lord will be delivered" (Joel 2:32).

8. *Selah* is the transliteration of this Hebrew word that is inserted repeatedly in the Psalms, mainly for the purpose of having the worshiper pause and consider the connection between the verse before and the verse after (Ps. 3:2).

9. Mankind began to make musical instruments on earth in the seventh generation (Gen. 4:21). King David made the musical instruments that were used in giving praise to God in the first temple (2 Chron. 7:6). Many of these no longer exist on earth, but those made by God in heaven exist forever (Rev. 8:13; 15:2).

10. The pavane was a majestic, processional, court dance in the sixteenth century, characterized by slow, formal movements. In southern Spain, it was performed in Christian churches on solemn occasions.

11. The throne of God in heaven is a literal and magnificent seat upon which the Father sits (Rev. 4:2–3; 5:7). The Bible records the testimony of six different people who saw Him sitting on His throne: five of them in visions (1 Kings 22:19; Isa. 6:1; Ezek. 1:26; Dan. 7:9; Rev. 21:5) and the sixth, Jesus Christ, who has lived there (Matt. 23:22).

12. There is "one God, the Father, from whom are all things" (1 Cor. 8:6). His nature is the source of true light (1 John 1:5; John 1:9; James 1:17). The form of the Father is light of incomparable whiteness similar to the glory manifested in Jesus on the Mount of Transfiguration (Mark 9:3; John 5:37). His light illumines all of heaven (Rev. 21:23).

13. God "looks to the ends of the earth and sees everything under the heavens" (Job 28:24). His eyes see every step taken by every person,

and He understands all their works (Job 34:21; Ps. 33:13, 15). He knows every person's attitude toward Him, for God "looks at the heart" (1 Sam. 16:7; Jer. 12:3).

14. The *Shekinah* is a Hebrew word meaning "resting" or "dwelling," and it refers to that manifestation of the reddish-gold radiance of God's presence when it rests or dwells among His people on earth. The root of *Shekinah* is the Hebrew word *shokhen,* meaning "neighbor" or "intimacy." God's glory appeared first to the Israelites in the midst of the cloud that went before them when they left Egypt (Exod. 13:21–22; 16:10).

15. Ezekiel and John compared the upper half of the radiant sphere of colors surrounding the Father on His throne to a glorious bow (Ezek. 1:28; Rev. 4:3). This aspect of the light of His glory God calls "My bow," and the rainbow represents it on earth (Gen. 9:13, 16).

16. "The heavens are telling of the glory of God; and their expanse is declaring the work of His hands" (Ps. 19:1). God created and arranged the stars and constellations to picture the gospel of salvation in Christ. Another luminous phenomenon seen in the night sky, particularly in the northern arctic region, is called the aurora borealis. It appears in streamers of light ascending in the shape of a fan or as an arc of light across the sky from east to west.

17. The light of God is part of His nature (1 John 1:5). Therefore it is alive, active, and powerful like His Word (Heb. 4:12). It will transform the darkness of sin, sickness, and death in the natural person into the light that is Christ (John 12:46; Eph. 5:8).

18. Ezekiel heard the flight of heavenly beings whose wings emitted sounds on certain occasions. Some of these sounds were like the voice of God Almighty, like many waters, like the tumult in an army camp, and like a great rumbling (Ezek. 1:24; 3:12–13; 10:5). We see by this that their flying can produce many kinds of sounds.

19. When one is in the presence of the Lord, there is fullness of joy (Ps. 16:11). We come into His courts (His nearer presence) with the offering of sacrifices of praise, the psalmist says (Ps. 27:6; 96:8; 100:4). God creates the praise within us, and we give it to Him (Isa; 57:19; 2 Chron. 7:6). In return, He imparts His joy to us (Neh. 12:27, 43; Ps. 71:23).

20. The Bible describes the sound of the wings of heavenly beings in flight

as "like the voice of God Almighty when He speaks" (Ezek. 10:5). The speaking of God penetrates and becomes a part of believers (Ezek. 3:10; Job 22:22). In the original text of Psalm 109:4, David said of himself, "But I am prayer," in the same way that he described himself as "I am peace" (Ps. 120:7). Christ can impart both His prayer and peace to us by the Holy Spirit (Rom. 8:6, 26–27, 34; Eph. 2:14; 6:18; Col. 3:15; John 15:16).

21. The nearer we come into the presence of the person of the Father in heaven, the clearer our spiritual sight and our perception of spiritual realities become. Moses was able to see the glory of the goodness of His character (Exod. 33:18–19; 34:5–6). Isaiah saw the depth of his and others' sin (Isa. 6:5). Ezekiel knew the living beings to be cherubim (Ezek. 10:20). John heard all creation praising God (Rev. 5:13).

22. In the wilderness tabernacle, the golden altar of incense stood in front of the veil separating the holy of holies from the holy place (Exod. 40:26–27). Here was burned the holy incense that represents the prayers of the saints (Rev. 5:8). The true altar of incense is before the throne of God in heaven (Rev. 8:3).

23. Some of the earthly praises of the saints have to pass through the fire on the altar of incense that is before the throne to be purified before going to the Father (Rev. 8:4).

24. There are certain angels who stand in the immediate presence of God (Luke 1:19). John saw "the seven angels who stand before God" (Rev. 8:2). Paul indicates that there are certain angels who are chosen to stand in His presence (1 Tim. 5:21). Jesus spoke of these angels when He said, "I will confess [the believer's] name before My Father and His angels" (Rev. 3:5). The angels at the altar of incense are among those who attend upon the Father in close proximity. Their pale purple robes with deep purple and gold embroidery indicate that they are in the retinue of the divine king.

25. All things are from the Father, and all things are to Him (Rom. 11:36). Sin had separated all things from being able to return to the Father, but through Christ He reconciled all things to Himself, "having made peace through the blood of His cross" (Col. 1:20).

26. The sweet aroma around the throne area is due to several aspects of Christ Jesus, who is the fragrance to God (2 Cor. 2:15): His prayers, His praises, the sacrificial offering of Himself to the Father (Num. 28:2; Eph. 5:2), the odor from the mountains of spices of His perfec-

tions (Song of Sol. 8:14), and the manifestation of Christ's triumph in the redeemed (2 Cor. 2:14).

27. There is a oneness to everything created in heaven because everything originates from the Father through the Son by the Holy Spirit. Therefore, the nature of everything living in the kingdom of heaven is spirit (1 Cor. 15:50). That which is produced by the Spirit is spirit (John 3:6; 1 Pet. 2:5; Eph. 1:3). As a result, there is a oneness to the sight, sound, and odor there.

28. These flames of fire are manifestations of the Holy Spirit (Acts 2:3; Matt. 3:11–12) before the Father's throne (Rev. 4:5; 1:4). The fullness of the Holy Spirit in His sevenfold perfection is in Jesus Christ (Isa. 11:2; Rev. 3:1; 5:6) and Christ in Him (John 16:14).

29. Fire is a part of the holy being of God the Father and represents the absolute purity of the righteous perfection that is His alone (Isa. 5:16). Of all creatures, the fiery beings called seraphim most closely witness to the holiness of God. This order of heavenly beings, the plural of *saraph,* is a Hebrew word derived from a root meaning "to burn." They are described in the Scriptures only in the vision to Isaiah where they testify to the purity of His righteousness by their words extolling His holy name (Isa. 6:3) and by the fire of God purifying the lips of the prophet so that he might speak His holy words (Isa. 6:5–7). It therefore follows that the singing of the seraphim should be the sweetest and purest known to mankind.

30. The twenty-four beings around the throne of the Father are called "elders," a term signifying the governmental authority of those of faithful seniority. Their delegated rulership is seen in their wearing golden crowns, which at times they cast before the throne and prostrate themselves in worship (Rev. 4:4, 10). They praise God in song and speech, play instruments, and present the prayers of the saints before God (Rev. 5:8–9). An element of their authority, the one that is mainly portrayed in the Book of Revelation, is to humbly lead in worship (Rev. 5:8, 11). Many scholars believe that these elders are the eldest angels who assist in the administration of the other angels and in some way the administration of the universe for God.

31. Closer to the throne than the elders are the four living creatures described in Revelation 4:6–8. These four "give glory and honor and thanks" in praise to the Father on behalf of all of His created beings (Rev. 4:9, 11). They are covered with eyes, indicating a completeness of discernment through spiritual perception with understanding (2

Kings 6:17; Acts 26:18; 1 Cor. 2:9–10, 12, 14). They are one form of several kinds of cherubim, an order of heavenly beings who are mainly assigned to honor and guard the radiant glory of God wherever it is (Ezek. 9:3; 10:18–20). The cherubim in one vision to Ezekiel said, "Blessed be the glory of the LORD in His place" (Ezek. 3:12–13).

32. There are times when the redeemed take the initiative by the Spirit and begin to worship before the throne, and the angelic host joins in (Rev. 7:9–12).

33. The four living creatures and the twenty-four elders hold before God "golden bowls full of incense, which are the prayers of the saints" (Rev. 5:8). These prayers are first placed on the golden altar of incense before the throne, and they are also offered to God in incense burned by angels in a golden censer (Rev. 8:3–4).

34. They represent four great divisions of animate creation: the wild beasts, the lion; the domesticated beasts, the calf; humanity, the man; and the birds, the eagle. God includes these four categories of creatures with breath in the covenant He made with Noah and his sons after the flood (Gen. 9:8–10).

35. All things were created to praise the living God, as Psalm 148 enunciates. (See also Psalm 48:10; 69:34; 100:1.)

36. The heavenly beings declare their agreement with the praise of the redeemed in heaven (Rev. 7:9–12).

# Chapter 11

## The Father's Lap

1. The modern recorder is a type of flute with eight finger holes. The Bible says that the sound of the flute brings rejoicing and gladness of heart (Job 21:12; Isa. 30:29; 1 Kings 1:40).

2. The Father designed flowers to show forth the glorious aspects of the beauty of His Son. The flowers and all living things in heaven do not wither or die, for "everything that God does will remain forever" (Eccles. 3:14).

3. The Bible repeatedly shows us that God the Father has hands of light in the form of human hands with fingers. Examples of the use of His hands are writing with His finger (Exod. 31:18), covering someone with His hand (Exod. 33:22–23), touching someone's lips (Jer. 1:9), handing someone a cup of wine (Jer. 25:15), putting a scroll into someone's mouth (Ezek. 3:2), and picking up someone by his hair (Ezek. 8:3).

4. If God counts the number of the millions upon millions of stars and calls them all by their names (Ps. 147:4; Isa. 40:26), then surely He knows the name of every human being. He has recorded the names of His redeemed children in the "book of life of the Lamb" (Rev. 13:8).

5. The English word *mystery* is from the Greek word *musterion,* which means "a sacred secret that only God can reveal." He has been unveiling His mysteries in Scripture beginning in Genesis. In Christ Jesus "are hidden all the treasures of wisdom and knowledge," for He is the full understanding of all the mysteries of God (Col. 2:2–3). The Lord revealed many of these secrets of God to His disciples (Matt. 13:11) and to Paul (Eph. 3:2–5). He promised that He would make more known about the Father's name—His character and work (John 16:25; 17:26).

6. The Holy Spirit must breathe upon the speck of an embryo in the womb for it to have a human spirit and begin to live (Gen. 7:22; Zech. 12:1; John 6:63). From its beginning, a human spirit has all of its faculties for hearing and deciding about God (Ps. 22:10; 58:3; Isa. 49:1, 5; Jer. 1:5).

7. While in his mother's womb, John the Baptist was filled with the

Holy Spirit, and he leaped for joy when the Spirit spoke through the virgin Mary to his mother (Luke 1:15, 44).

8. "The Spirit searches all things, even the depths of God...the thoughts of God no one knows except the Spirit of God" (1 Cor. 2:10–11).

9. As Jesus and Stephen were dying, they asked the Father to forgive their murderers (Luke 23:34; Acts 7:60). The Word says, "Love your enemies, do good to those who hate you...pray for those who mistreat you" (Luke 6:27–28). We are also told to "overcome evil with good" (Rom. 12:21).

   The leaves of the henna tree yield a red dye; the Hebrew word for this tree means "a redemption price," deriving from a root word meaning "to forgive."

10. God knows the children who will be aborted, miscarried, or die too young to be able to choose the Lord Jesus, so the Holy Spirit presents that choice to these in the womb. All those who believe in Him will go to heaven when they die (John 6:39–40).

11. The letters of the Hebrew root word for *cherub* mean "holding something in safe keeping." The two cherubim on either side of God's throne serve as an honor guard or "chariot" to uphold the glory of the Creator of all (1 Chron. 28:18; 2 Sam. 22:1). The Bible refers to cherubim as those above whom the Father "sits" or "is enthroned" (Ps. 99:1, literal Hebrew; 80:1). They are a composite of the four categories of living creatures because God created them to live in harmony together (Gen. 2:19) before sin shattered their unity (Gen. 9:2; Hos. 4:2–3). The man is the head of these composite cherubim because he was ordained to rule for God over the other animate creation (Gen. 1:28). These two "cherubim of glory" (Heb. 9:5) were represented on earth by the golden figures on either end of the mercy seat in the tabernacle where God met and spoke with Moses (Exod. 25:18, 21–22).

12. The throne of God is resplendent with the most valuable of all: the divine character and virtues of the Father. These comprise His authority and that by which He rules. Righteousness and justice are the foundation of His throne (Ps. 97:2). He is righteous and just (Ps. 11:7; Zech. 9:9). He loves righteousness and justice (Ps. 33:5). He works righteousness and justice (Ps. 99:4).

13. True gold, like every created thing in heaven, is transparent because it exists to be illumined by God's glory (Rev. 21:18, 21, 23).

14. Jesus said that His Father has a "form," a figure or shape that can be seen (John 5:37). Many people saw His bodily form: Moses alone (Num. 12:8) and again with all the leaders of Israel (Exod. 24:9–11). The body of the Son of God is like His Father's appearance, for the Son is in His image (2 Cor. 4:4; Phil. 2:6; Col. 2:9). Jesus said, "He who has seen Me has seen the Father" (John 14:9).

15. The divine light that is of God flashes through His garment in heaven like lightning as an indication of His awesome power (Rev. 4:5; 16:18). The power of the Lord Jesus on earth also permeated His garment (Luke 8:43–46; 6:19).

16. No human being can see the brightness of the glory of God's face and live through the experience (Exod. 33:20; 1 Tim. 6:16). Angels are able to behold His countenance (Matt. 18:10), and believers in their resurrected bodies will see His face (Rev. 22:4).

17. The primary Hebrew word translated "to worship" literally means "to bow down," not a matter of words or feelings but an act of humbling oneself. An example is Moses in the presence of the glory of God's grace (Exod. 34:8). When the glory cloud of God filled the temple, none of the ministering priests were able to stand (1 Kings 8:10–11).

18. The same words translated "lap" in both Testaments are also translated "bosom." When one sits, the lap is almost the equivalent of the bosom. This represents the intimacy that the Son has "in the bosom of the Father" (John 1:18).

19. The Lord has made His disciples to be "a kingdom, priests to His God and Father" (Rev. 1:6). Priests are chosen and brought near to God to dwell in His courts (Ps. 65:4). God gave His covenant of peace to the Aaronic priesthood through Phinehas (Num. 25:11–13). The Melchizedek priesthood of those who have believed into Jesus includes a greater covenant of peace (Heb. 7:17, 24). Christ is their peace (Eph. 2:14).

20. Christ Jesus is our hope of drawing near to God the Father and to dwell in Him with His Son even while we still walk the earth (1 Tim. 1:1; Heb. 7:19; John 17:21; Col. 3:3; Rev. 3:12). He is "a hope both sure and steadfast and one which enters within the veil, where [He] has entered as a forerunner for us" (Heb. 6:19–20). Having entered within the veil in spirit, "we look not at the things which are seen, but at the things which are not seen" (2 Cor. 4:18). Our desires and minds are set on "things above, not on the things that are on earth" (Col. 3:2).

21. "Delight yourself in the LORD, and He will give you the desires of your heart" (Ps. 37:4). If we "[desist] from [our] own ways, from seeking our [own] pleasure, and speaking [our] own word, then [we] will take delight in the Lord" (Isa. 58:13–14). He will move us beyond the heights of the earth by drawing us after Him (Song of Sol. 1:4; John 6:44).

22. The Lord God dwelt within a dark cloud when He visited the Israelites at Mount Sinai (Exod. 19:9; Deut. 4:11; Ps. 18:9).

23. "[No one knows] who the Father is except the Son, and anyone to whom the Son wills to reveal Him" (Luke 10:22). "He who has seen Me has seen the Father," Jesus said (John 14:9).

24. One meaning of "waters" in Scripture is "peoples and multitudes and nations and tongues" (Rev. 17:15). Troubled waters symbolize heathen peoples in an uproar (2 Chron. 15:6). Jesus said that there would be "dismay among nations, in perplexity at the roaring of the sea and the waves, men fainting from fear and the expectation of the things which are coming upon the world" (Luke 21:25–26).

25. The more the judgments of God come upon the earth at the end of the age, the more clearly His glory will appear upon His children. They will begin to "shine forth as the sun in the kingdom of their Father" (Matt. 13:43; Isa. 60:1–2).

26. God has ordained that the salvation of the Lord Jesus be carried out on earth with the free consent and cooperation of those in the one body of His Son, those who have been made a part of the risen Christ (Eph. 1:22–23; 2:16; 3:10; 5:23, 25–27, 30).

27. "Open your mouth and eat what I am giving you" (Ezek. 2:8). "Thy words were found and I ate them; and Thy words became for me a joy and the delight of my heart" (Jer. 15:16). "Write in a book what you see...and the things which are, and the things which will take place after these things" (Rev. 1:11, 19). "Blessed is he who reads and those who hear the words [with understanding]...and heed the things which are written in it; for the time is near" (Rev. 1:3).

28. The word *chancellor* is from the Late Latin *cancellarius*, meaning a doorkeeper or a secretary to a king. God's chancellor is one who opens the door for others to come to know Him through a written record of proceedings in heaven and their substantiation by the Scriptures. As the risen Lord opened the minds of the eleven apostles and those who

were with them to understand the things concerning Himself in all the Bible, now He is opening the mind of His church to deeper revelation of the Father's heart (Luke 24:27, 33, 45; John 16:12–13, 25).

29. The hope of returning to heaven, our true home, to know our true Father, our true Brother, and our true Friend, the Holy Spirit, lies deep within the new, human, spiritual heart (Ezek. 36:26; John 17:3; 2 Cor. 5:8; Phil. 1:23). The resurrected spirit of each believer is already there in Christ (1 Cor. 6:17; Eph. 2:5–6; John 12:26; 17:24).

30. God knew each of us in Christ before we were born into the world (Jer. 1:5; Ps. 139:16). "He chose us in Him before the foundation of the world" and called us according to His purpose (Eph. 1:4; Rom. 8:29–30; Gal. 1:15).

31. Human wisdom and the reasonings of worldly thinkers are useless nonsense to God (1 Cor. 1:20; 3:20). "God has mainly chosen the foolish people...the weak...the lowly and despised, even those considered nonentities, in order to nullify those who think themselves to be somebodies—so that no one may boast before Him" (1 Cor. 1:27–29, paraphrased).

32. The Father delights in one He has called to fulfill His purposes because of the apportionment of the grace of His Son's character, life, and ministry that He chooses to allot to that person (Gal. 5:22–23; Rom. 12:3, 6; 1 Cor. 12:7, 11; Eph. 4:7, 15–16).

33. The Father has placed His entire trust in His Son, giving Him all authority to bring all creation to completion (John 3:35; Matt. 28:18; Eph. 1:22). The Son warrants this trust because He laid Himself aside from eternity out of love for His Father, in order to fully obey and manifest His Father rather than Himself (Phil. 2:6–8; John 5:19, 30).

34. There is nothing good and trustworthy dwelling in the natural state in which we were born, that is, in our "flesh," which hates God and refuses to obey Him (Rom. 1:30; 8:7). Christ Jesus is the only good and trustworthy thing in us, for He has been made all things for us from God (1 Cor. 1:30; Col. 3:11).

35. The natural expression of the earthly person in soul and body, called in Scripture "the old self" (Eph. 4:22; Col. 3:9) or "himself" (Matt. 16:24), must be denied and laid aside as worthless to God. The Holy Spirit will enable us to keep it incapacitated on the individual cross

that He provides each of us, as Jesus bears His personal one (Matt. 16:24). The life of God in Christ alone is to be manifested in us (Eph. 4:24; 2 Cor. 4:10–11). The natural or old person cannot be changed, for it is hopelessly centered on itself rather than God. Christians change only by having more of Christ Jesus, the one new man, formed in them (Gal. 4:19; Eph. 2:15; 4:13).

36. God the Spirit causes believers to grow up together in all aspects into Christ (Col. 2:19; Eph. 4:15): in His salvation by the Scriptures (1 Pet. 2:2), in the grace of faith and love and of the knowledge of Him (2 Thess. 1:3; 2 Pet. 3:18), and in being fitted together into a holy temple in the Lord (Eph. 2:21).

37. In the End Time, God's family will be restored to Him (Mal. 4:5–6; Eph. 3:14–15; Mark 9:12) from the captivity of a double heart (Ps. 12:2), so that they no longer go limping between two opinions (1 Kings 18:21, KJV). The Father is unveiling more of His heart so His people may know that He has turned their heart back again (1 Kings 18:37) and that He has given them a heart to know and understand Him (Deut. 29:4; Matt. 13:15) and that they may love Him with all their heart (Deut. 4:29).

38. Whirling wheels accompany certain cherubim (Ezek. 1:15–20; 10:13).

39. When God created the earth, the host of heaven "sang together and...shouted for joy" (Job 38:7; Rev. 12:4, "stars of heaven"; Job 1:6, "sons of God").

40. The trumpets were blown in heaven on this occasion for one of the same reasons that the two silver trumpets in Israel were sounded to gather everyone together: to rejoice in worshiping God in His immediate presence (Num. 10:2–3, 10).

41. The Israelites usually used a trumpet made of a ram's horn called a *shofar*, the transliteration of the Hebrew *shophar*. One of the purposes of their blowing the shofar is the same as that for which it was blown now in heaven: to solemnly prepare everyone for a new revelation or act by God (Exod. 19:13; Josh. 6:5; Joel 2:15).

# Chapter 12

## The Installation

1. Thunder, lightning, and fire coming from the Father are part of the manifestations of His presence. Often in Scripture they indicate that He is going to speak or act. This was true before He spoke the Ten Commandments to the children of Israel on Mount Sinai (Exod. 19:16–18; Job 36:33).

2. All belongs to the Father (Job 41:11). When the Father draws a person to His Son (John 6:44) and that one is born again of the Spirit, he is given to the Son to be brought to resurrection (John 6:39) and finally to be returned to the Father (1 Cor. 15:24; Eph. 1:4). The Lord Jesus confesses the name of His own before the Father and His angels (Rev. 3:5).

3. The Lord Jesus quoted His Father's words spoken to Moses: "By the mouth of two or three witnesses every fact may be confirmed" (Matt. 18:16; Deut. 19:15).

4. The number twelve signifies the perfection of government: the twelve patriarchs and the twelve apostles. Twice twelve, or twenty-four, expresses heavenly government or leadership. Twenty-four insignias on one chain represent the heavenly authority delegated to one in an office of responsibility.

5. The new, spiritual heart is the vital life link between the hidden, inner person and the outer person (Prov. 4:23; 1 Pet. 3:4; 2 Cor. 4:16).

6. The wearing of the cloak or mantle (chapter 5, note 1) signifies spiritual anointing for a ministry of the Lord Jesus to be exercised through a believer. Such was the passing of Elijah's mantle to Elisha (1 Kings 19:19; 2 Kings 2:9, 13–15).

7. From the gospel account of what Jesus did on earth, we learn what His Father does in heaven (John 5:19–20). We therefore know that one reason God the Father lays His hand upon someone is to initiate a supernatural work in them as Christ did: healing (Luke 22:51), strengthening (Rev. 1:17), or blessing (Mark 10:16).

8. God's name placed on one's forehead indicates His ownership and

the impartation of the spiritual capacity to know Him (Rev. 14:1; 22:4).

9. A scepter is a short staff borne by a king as an emblem of authority. The strong scepter of the Lord Jesus was stretched forth from Zion (Ps. 110:2), a scepter of uprightness (Ps. 45:6).

10. The Holy Spirit, proceeding from the Father through the Son, bears witness of the Son's witness (John 15:26; 16:13).

11. In the same way that human elders represent the church when they lay their hands upon a believer to impart graces and giftings (1 Cor. 1:3; Acts 8:14–17), so the angelic elders represent the heavenly host as they bestow such blessings.

12. All things that the Father has belong to His Son (John 16:15). The children of God are also fellow heirs of the Father with Christ (Rom. 8:16–17).

13. Another reason God lays His hand upon someone is to designate that person as belonging to Him (Ezek. 3:14; Phil. 3:12). He alone gives the measure of the faith, hope, and love of His Son by the Holy Spirit to the spiritual heart of His children (Eph. 3:17–19; 1 Tim. 1:1). The three Persons of the Trinity are meant to dwell there, for the new heart belongs to them (John 14:23; Gal. 4:6).

14. The fire of the Spirit of God tests the quality of the way we use our eyes, and it burns up the chaff (Matt. 3:12; 1 Cor. 3:13). The fire of the finger of God, the Holy Spirit, also casts out any darkness from the work of the enemy that may be present in us (Luke 11:20; Matt. 6:23).

15. Great power issued forth through the hands of Jesus Christ when He laid them upon the eyes of the blind (Mark 8:25). God "covers His hands with the lightning [His power], and commands it to strike the mark" (Job 36:32).

16. One of the seraphim touched the lips of the prophet Isaiah with a burning coal from the altar in heaven, declaring his iniquity removed and his sin forgiven (Isa. 6:6–7).

17. Shoulders symbolize strength to carry responsibility (Isa. 9:6). God's right hand touching both shoulders of a person confers power and blessing (Gen. 48:17–18; Mark 14:62). We carry the shield of faith with one hand and the sword of God's Word with the other (Eph. 6:16–17).

18. These words speak of the humility of God: "I bent down and fed them [His people]" (Hos. 11:4). We see the Son's humble heart in His kneeling to wash the disciples' feet (John 13:4–5).

19. The sword is the living, moving, powerful, Spirit-energized Word of God concerning Christ Jesus that reveals the true condition of our spiritual hearts (Heb. 4:12–13). It is truth as it is in Jesus, and it overcomes the lies of the enemy (Eph. 4:21; 6:17; Rev. 12:11).

20. Scripture describes cherubim with one, two, or four faces (Ezek. 1:10; 41:18; Rev. 4:7). In the vision of a new temple, there were cherubim with the faces of a man and of a lion carved on the walls (Ezek. 41:19). The Lord Jesus is "the Lion that is from the tribe of Judah" (Rev. 5:5).

21. The sword of God's Word is empowered by the Holy Spirit who takes that which is of Christ Jesus and discloses it to those who are one with Him (John 16:14; 1 Cor. 6:17).

22. The sword of the God's Word in our hearts can be wielded by the Spirit through our actions (hands) or spoken by the Spirit through our mouths (Matt. 10:19–20; Col. 3:17). That Word wars against the enemy and strengthens the brethren (Rom. 12:21; Eph. 6:17–19; Col. 3:16; Rev. 2:16).

23. There are many books that God the Holy Spirit has written personally (Exod. 32:32; Dan. 7:10) with His fiery-red pen and golden ink. Examples are the book of life (Rev. 20:12), the book of the days ordained for each person (Ps. 139:16), the book of our tears (Ps. 56:8), the book of those recorded for life in Jerusalem (Isa. 4:3), and a book of remembrance of those who fear God and esteem His name (Mal. 3:16).

24. "The Spirit of truth...proceeds from the Father" through the Son (John 15:26). "The Spirit of truth...will not speak on His own initiative, but whatever He hears, He will speak" (John 16:13).

25. The Spirit of truth as it is in Jesus sets us free (John 8:31–32): from bondage to sin (Rom. 6:12–14), self (Rom. 6:6), and the world (Gal. 6:14); from oppression (Isa. 10:27); from the prison of darkness (Ps. 107:10–14); from sickness (Luke 13:16); from the law (Gal. 5:1–4); and from death (John 11:25–26).

26. The two large pillars supporting the roof over the porch of the temple

that Solomon built were named Jachin, "He establishes," and Boaz, "In Him is strength" (1 Kings 7:15, 21). In the spiritual sense, the pillars stood guard at the entrance to the holy place, as cherubim also guarded the entrance to the Garden of Eden (Gen. 3:24).

27. David, Solomon's father, said that God made him understand all the plan for the temple to be built, including the porch, "in writing by His [the Holy Spirit's] hand upon me" (1 Chron. 28:11, 19). The two cherubim named Jachin and Boaz are assigned to stand guard over the revelation of the words of God in writing by the inspiration of the Holy Spirit.

28. The whirlwind is a visible representation of the powerful moving of the Holy Spirit as on the day of Pentecost "like a violent, rushing wind" (Acts 2:2). The Greek word for *wind* in John 3:8 is the same word that is translated "Spirit" in the New Testament.

29. At times there is silence in heaven, as when the seventh seal is broken, with the host there waiting to behold what God would do (Rev. 8:1). "It is good that [one] waits silently for the salvation of the Lord" (Lam. 3:26).

30. The hands of a believer represent the visible work (Matt. 5:16). The feet stand for the walk or conduct that is seen (2 Cor. 4:2). The head is the place of spoken thoughts (1 Cor. 2:11–13). The Holy Spirit reveals only Christ, not Himself, and He does the same thing in the believer.

31. A porpoise skin covering over the tabernacle in the wilderness hid its true purpose from the eyes of the world (Exod. 26:14).

32. Jesus as the Christ was hidden from recognition except by divine revelation (Luke 10:21). The believer's life is hidden in God (Col. 3:3), so that only Christ Jesus in him may be manifested (2 Cor. 4:10–11).

33. Jesus said that "whoever wishes to save his life [Greek *psuche,* the expression of his own soul] shall lose it [when he dies], and whoever loses his life [soul] for My sake [so as to express My soul], he is the one who will save it [for eternity]" (Luke 9:24).

34. Everyone in heaven is without shoes, for all the ground there is holy (Acts 7:33).

35. Jesus rebuked those who justified themselves, seeking to be consid-

ered righteous in the sight of people (Luke 16:15) rather than before God, who alone is the One who declares us righteous in His Son (Rom. 8:33).

36. Part of the individual cross, which is continually offered to each believer, works the invisibility to others of one's self (Luke 14:27; Eph. 4:22).

37. An exposed heel means anything in one's walk (behavior) that makes one vulnerable to being wounded or tripped up by the enemy (Gen. 3:15; Matt. 18:7; 1 Cor. 3:3; 1 Pet. 5:8–10).

38. A strong ankle is needed to walk well. A spiritual walk is behavior that rests upon supernatural faith in and manifestation of the Lord Jesus in love (John 6:29; 15:5; Eph. 5:2). Only the Holy Spirit can bring this forth (Gal. 5:16). He strengthens us to be able to allow Christ to be and do this in His strength (Phil. 4:13).

39. Nothing good dwells in or originates from our "flesh," the earthly person (Rom. 7:18). On the cross God removed all spiritual life-support to this old self (Rom. 6:6).

40. The functioning of the natural person can only produce spiritual death (Rom. 8:6, 13).

41. Jesus said, "I do not receive glory [honor or fame] from men.... How can you believe [trust in God] when you receive [and trust in] glory from one another, and you do not seek the glory that is from the one and only God?" (John 5:41, 44). The rulers of His day "loved the approval of men rather than the approval of God" (John 12:43).

42. God maintains a sufficient degree of freedom in our will to enable us to choose for or against Him in every matter. He respects that freedom and waits for us to be willing. "Whosoever will, let him take the water of life freely" (Rev. 22:17, KJV).

43. "I do believe; help my unbelief," the father of the epileptic boy cried out to Jesus (Mark 9:24).

44. The "great fire" of the jealous, holy love of the Father infuses and envelops Him (Deut. 4:24, 36), as it does His throne (Dan. 7:9). The whole top of Mount Sinai was enveloped by His fire (Exod. 24:17).

45. "God thunders with His voice wondrously" (Job 37:5).

46. "Who among us can live with the consuming fire?" (Isa. 33:14).

47. The Scriptures speak plainly of a place within God the Father (the Greek *en,* translated "in," means "into or within") where the believer may live in spirit and may fellowship with Him and His Son. An example is: "God [the Father] is light.... If we walk in [within] the light... we have fellowship with one another [the Father and the believer]" (1 John 1:5–7). The conditions for a saint to abide within God the Father and His Son (and They in him) are to abide in His love and in His Word (John 14:23; 1 John 2:24). As the Son abides in the Father, so we are to be perfected into the oneness that They have (John 15:10; 17:21–23), for the Son has prepared this place for us (John 14:3; 17:24).

48. Ezekiel saw visions of "burning coals of fire" (Ezek. 1:13; 10:2) and of something like fire near the form of God (Ezek. 1:27).

49. These projectiles of God's fire were to purify and to intensify the spiritual perception.

50. God is a consuming fire (Deut. 4:24). By His Word He burns up the refuse in us and infuses the remainder with the burning purity of His love (Jer. 23:29; Matt. 3:11–12; Heb. 12:27–29).

51. The fire of God must burn within the inner person (spiritual heart and human spirit—1 Pet. 3:4) as well as the outer person (2 Cor. 4:16) of the soul expressed through the body.

52. The Lord Jesus' eyes are "a flame of fire" (Rev. 1:14; 2:18–19). These eyes indicate His intuitive knowledge through the "eyes of [His] heart" (Eph. 1:18), the same way that the Father knows all things by "the eyes of [His] heart."

53. Paul prays that the Father would give the saints to know intuitively with the eyes (perception with understanding) of their hearts as God knows (Eph. 1:17–18).

54. The Father looks with compassion and mercy upon His people and the lost, as Jesus did on earth (Mark 5:19; 6:34).

55. "Whoever speaks, let him speak, as it were, the utterances of God" (1 Pet. 4:11).

56. Divine love is "the very flame of the Lord [God]," the burning, all-

consuming, everlasting passion of His heart (Song of Sol. 8:6; Jer. 31:3).

57. Many are invited to walk with God as Enoch did, in oneness here on earth, but few are chosen because the path of living by His life is a narrow one (Gen. 5:24; Matt. 7:14; 22:2–5, 14; John 6:57; 17:21; Col. 3:3). Few will enter it (Matt. 7:14). Fewer yet will go all the way (Phil. 2:20–21; 3:12–14). At every stage of sanctification, God must call each of us, saying, "Seek My face" (Ps. 27:8). If we freely respond, He will choose us to receive the grace for His Son to be and do that in us (2 Tim. 1:9).The Father zealously yearns for His children to put His Son both as a seal over their hearts so that they will be completely His (2 Chron. 16:9) and as a seal on their arm (He is their strength—Ps. 18:1): that they may become an unquenchable flame of His love on earth (Song of Sol. 8:7) and within Him in heaven (Rev. 3:12).

58. Scripture describes Christ's love for His Father as four dimensional, the fourth being expansion or growth (Eph. 3:18). Divine love is ever abounding (Exod. 34:6) in the Lord Jesus (Eph. 3:19) and in those joined to Him (Phil. 1:9; 1 Thess. 3:12).

# Conclusion

## The Return

1. The Hebrew word translated *Mahanaim* means "two camps." This is the name Jacob gave the place where he and his household camped and where the angels also camped (Gen. 32:1–2). In another context it is the name of a dance of two companies (Song of Sol. 6:13).

2. To enter the fire of God involves a burning to ashes of that which is not of Him, in the way that silver or gold is refined (Zech. 13:9; Mal. 3:3; Ezek. 22:18; 1 Cor. 3:11–15; 1 Pet. 1:7).

3. The Father shared His heart with His friends like Abraham and Moses (Gen. 18:17; Exod. 33:11; Isa. 41:8). Jesus shared all that He heard from the Father with His friends (John 15:15).

4. The Father is able to act and speak through the radiant glory that surrounds His Person and is a visible form of His infinite goodness (Exod. 33:19). He causes this glory to appear or disappear (Exod. 16:10; Matt. 17:5), to move from one place to another (Ezek. 10:4; 11:23), to be reflected upon the face of a person (Exod. 34:29; 2 Cor. 3:7), and to transform His children from within (2 Cor. 3:18) as Jesus was changed on the mountain (Matt. 17:2). Believers bless in God's name by laying their hands in prayer upon the head of another (Gen. 48:14). God the Father may bless a believer by touching his forehead with His glory (Prov. 10:6).

5. The promise made by the Lord many years ago concerned seeing into heaven (chapter 2, note 3). He also promised the disciples around Him on earth that they would "see the heavens opened" (John 1:51).

6. Those portions of the Scripture that are made powerfully alive by the Holy Spirit to a believer pierce the depths of the individual's spiritual heart. There the Word divides or discerns between that which comes from his natural soul (mind, emotions, and will) and that which issues from his spirit (Heb. 4:12).

7. The earthly capacities of the soul (mind, emotions, and will) must be governed (2 Cor. 10:5), renewed (Eph. 4:23), and supplied by the Holy Spirit with Christ's soul life (Mark 8:35) through the new inner person (spiritual heart and spirit, 1 Pet. 3:4). The transformed soul

must govern the body, never the body controlling the soul. God's dealing with the body is a work of disciplining its members (such as the mouth, eyes, and ears) so that the saint presents them continually to be used to glorify God (Rom. 6:13; 12:1; 1 Cor. 6:20). There is a permanent law of sin in the body that prevents the independent use of its members from ever being redeemed (Rom. 7:23).

8. At the new birth, God gives us a new spiritual heart that is clean (Ps. 51:10; Ezek. 36:26). But it must be kept clean in the conscience part of it by confession of sins and by faith in the cleansing power of His blood (Heb. 9:14; 10:22; 1 John 1:7, 9; Acts 15:9).

9. Jesus said that "the worries of the world, and the deceitfulness of riches, and the desires for other things enter in [a person] and choke the word" from growing up in his heart and producing the fruit of Christ's character (Mark 4:18–19). The spirit in the prophet Elijah was undistracted by these idolatries.

10. The Holy Spirit in Elijah confronted the four hundred fifty false, idolatrous prophets in Israel and overcame them when the fire of God fell and consumed his offering. He had prayed "that this people may know that Thou, O LORD, art God, and Thou hast turned their heart back again" (1 Kings 18:18–40).

11. Within earthly oil is latent power to move the machinery of the world. There is literal oil (as there is literal water) that comes directly from the Holy Spirit, by whose power the Father accomplishes all His working (Gen. 1:2; 1 Cor. 2:4; 12:11). The anointing oil applied to the priests and to the articles of the tabernacle (Exod. 30:22–33) and the oil used in the golden lampstand (Exod. 27:20) were symbols of the true oil of the Holy Spirt (Song of Sol. 1:3; Ps. 45:7; 89:20).

# Biography

"Anna" is a husband-and-wife team.

After Albert Rountree's graduation from the seminary at Yale University, he spent most of his adult life in the pastoral ministry. Ann Rountree was a minister's wife.

Following Albert's retirement, the Lord called the couple to a large metropolitan area to help bring pastors together for monthly prayer gatherings. Pastors from over seventy denominations and diverse ethnic backgrounds participated. They also organized daily prayer meetings for intercessors across sectarian lines, that city's first Pastors' Prayer Summit, and its first March for Jesus.

They now live a quiet life apart with the Lord in the mountains of North Carolina.